MISTER MCHOTTIE

PIPPA GRANT

ABOUT

Mister McHottie
(A Billionaire Boss / Brothers' Best Friend / Enemies to
Lovers Romantic Comedy)

The Best Enemies Make the Best Lovers...

Chase

I've just bought the woman of my nightmares.

Technically, I bought the company she works for. Point is, she cost me my two best friends ten years ago. It's payback time, and I'm going to make her life hell.

When I'm not banging her silly and myself stupid.

I need to get my head back in business, because getting off is great, but *He was a man who had sex, and lots of it, and in the worst locations, with the woman of his nightmares* isn't the inscription I want on my tombstone.

Even if it's true.

Ambrosia

There are three things I hate:

Bratwurst in any form, my neighbors boinking loudly like farm animals at 3 AM, and Chase Jett.

Mostly I hate Chase Jett. It's been ten years since he took my virginity—I'd make a bratwurst joke, but the unfortunate truth is that it would have to be a bratbest joke, and yes, it kills me to admit it—and now he's not only a billionaire, he's also my new boss.

Turns out our hate is mutual. And this kind of hate is horrifically twisted, filthy, and banging hot.

I just might have to hate him forever.

Mister McHottie is 45,000 hilarious, hot, sexy words that your mother warned you about, complete with an organic happy-ever-after (or seven), a Bratwurst Wagon, ill-advised office pranks, and no cheating or cliffhangers.

Ambrosia May Berger (Bro for short, but only to her enemies)

IT's 3 AM and they're at it again. I grab my broom and bang on the ceiling. "Some of us have to work in a few hours, you jackrabbits!"

The _squeaky-squeaky-squeaky-squeeeeeeak_ of the bedsprings is followed by a long moan and a high-pitched, come-to-Jesus pig squeal.

Finally.

If I ever meet my upstairs neighbor, I will _not_ be able to look her in the snout.

Eye. I mean eye.

I might offer her some lube though.

For the squeaky bedsprings. Cross my heart.

I roll over in the relative quiet—the city is never fully quiet, which is one of the things I love about it—but I can't get back to sleep, because I said _work_, and now my mind is spinning. I'm a social media manager for Crunchy, the second-biggest organic grocery store in New York.

At least, I was yesterday. Tomorrow remains to be seen. Crunchy was just bought out by a soulless dickstool who hides baby powder in unsuspecting women's hairdryers and who hums the first few bars of "It's a Small World" to get it stuck in your ear for *days* and who makes innocent girls take the fall for—ahem.

Hold on. My official Crunchy social media manager hat is here somewhere... Ah, yes. There it is.

Right.

Crunchy has been acquired by an environmentally-conscious, self-made billionaire philanthropist who gives lollipops, puppies, and rainbows to orphans when he's not personally digging recyclables out of landfills.

It's not the official party line, but it's close. I toss to my other side, because I'm gagging now.

I've loved working at Crunchy since I landed in New York six years ago, but it's job hunting time. There are lots of companies in the city not owned by Chase Jett—or anyone else who knew me ten years ago—who would love to hire an experienced social media manager.

And one or two of them might not run a background check, so I might even stand a chance of getting through the hiring process.

Squeaky-squeaky-squeaky-squeeeeeeeeak...

I shove my head under the pillow, close my eyes, and start counting free-range sheep.

————

By 10 AM, I'm jacked up on four cups of organic, fair trade iced coffee—Crunchy brand, of course—and I still have nothing on Parker's emotional jitters.

My work bff is balancing on a yoga ball across the room in our open office at headquarters in Midtown, fingers clicking over her laptop as she texts me on our corporate internal messaging system. She's afraid she'll be on the chopping block when the inevitable company reorganization happens.

I snort softly to myself. More likely she'll get my job, probably by the end of today.

Parker's message pops up with a goth emoji as her profile picture, even though she's a freckled brunette with virgin hair that has never been touched by dyes or colors, chemical, organic, or any other way. She calls it being ironic. I call her adorable.

"I can't lose my job, Sia," the goth emoji Parker says. "I'm half a paycheck away from moving back in with my parents."

She's not the only one who's strapped for cash. At least three of my four employees are also living on a shoestring budget, including April, resident photographer in the marketing department who's currently arranging bok choy in a sustainable bamboo bowl for an upcoming feature about the leafy greens we grow in-house.

Seriously. We grow vegetables in our building. It's high-tech and super cool and I'm so pissed I could spit that it belongs to the Dick now.

"You'll be fine," I type back to Parker on my company-issued tablet. "We kick ass. Crunchy needs us."

Completely true. Also true? The Crunchy marketing department is a great place to work. Our office is open and airy, with couches and beanbag chairs and yoga balls instead of cubes. Modular desks line the walls for people who dig the traditional set-up, and we have a stock of every type of phone, tablet, and computer known to man accessible to us in the media room. Necessity when you're in modern marketing.

It's weird, but it works for us. And it works because we're a Crunchy family.

A family I need to leave soon.

Thanks, dickhead.

In the light of the day—and with the aid of the coffee—I've comforted myself with the probability that billionaire organic grocery store taker-over-ers don't make the rounds to meet all the employees. Or even a fraction of them. Which means I can wait a few days to hear back on a select few feelers I put out this morning before I resort to blindly sending resumes.

"I heard he's stopping by today," April says.

I fumble and almost drop the tablet I'm using to check customer comments on our Facebook page.

She shoots me a knowing grin, then tilts a light on the bok choy and looks at it through her Nikon again. "I also heard he can bench a Volkswagen. I'd shoot that."

I'd shoot him too, but not with a camera. "Better for our image if he benched a Tesla."

My sarcasm is lost on her. "That's brilliant. I'm putting it in the suggestion box."

"We can make life-size cardboard cut-outs for all our stores," chimes in Madison. She writes the copy for our posts and single-handedly tripled sales of chickpeas with her *Funnust Hummust* series last year. I'd forgive her for the idea of wasting good cardboard if she were putting anyone but the Dick on it. "*Fueled by Crunchy.* New slogan. I call dibs on putting it in the box." A rare frown draws her dark brows together. "He won't change the employee suggestion box, will he? I like the suggestion box."

Wouldn't be the worst he's ever done.

Four sets of eyeballs swivel my way, and I realize I just said that out loud. "Didn't his date wear fur to some charity auction last year?" I say quickly.

I have no idea. For the last decade, he hasn't existed to me. I don't think about him, my family doesn't talk about him, and none of my friends know I know him. But my offhand suggestion sends half the social media department scurrying to Google, which gives me a minute to breathe and re-focus.

Think of kittens. And cupcakes. And kittens in party hats made from recycled cardboard posing with cupcakes.

Cake doesn't have to be made from organic flour, natural food dyes, fair trade cocoa, and free-range eggs.

Cake is cake is cake.

I'm deciding to have a slice of cake for lunch—chocolate, of course, from this *oh my god amazing* not at all organic bakery two blocks away because today's a triple fudge frosting kind of day, plus if I bought a slice of cake at the snack bar here, some of my money would go directly into the Dick's pockets—when the oak door squeaks open.

A moment of deathly silence is shattered by a flurry of squeals that would give my neighbor's bedsprings stiff competition. *Stiff*, heh, look at that, I can still make a bad joke today.

Every single member of the social media department lunges for *something*. April turns her camera to the door and goes paparazzi. Madison tries to hide behind an Apple Watch before she bends her head so her short dark hair covers her face. Parker's fingers go so fast over her keyboard there's smoke, and the *ding* of her message on my tablet rings over every other sound in the room.

Six feet of pure sin stands wide-legged in the doorway. His smile is a lie, his smoky blue eyes a portal to self-destruction, the dimple in his chin twice the size needed to store what's left of his conscience.

My eyes betray me and drift to his corded arms—I'm a sucker for a guy in gray suit pants with the sleeves of his white button-down shirt rolled up his forearms—and I can see Madison's right.

He probably *could* bench a Volkswagen.

Damn him.

There's a wave of palpable energy when he strolls in flanked by Rod Xavier, VP of Marketing, and a host of other suits who are either lackeys or wannabes.

I turn my back, bury myself in a beanbag chair, and slip on my headphones. Social media waits for no billionaire, and we have bok choy to sell.

That's when I notice the message from Goth Parker. "Is it too much to offer to have his babies?"

"Sexual harassment will get you fired," I shoot back.

"Jeez, who put insecticide in your mangoes this morning?"

My fingers hover over the keyboard, the truth threatening to spill out. Sweat is gathering in the bottom of my bra.

No one here knows I'm from Wishberry Lake, Minnesota, home of canned baloney, pineapple tater tot casserole, and the Fighting Dandelions high school football team. It's Minnesota. Don't judge.

Also from Wishberry Lake?

Chase Jett.

Number One Dick on my Dick List. He's the reason I tell people I'm from Pittsburgh. I hope when they put him up at Madame Tussaud's, they use ear wax. I hope when he goes on *Naked and Afraid*, they release him in the wilds of Minnesota and someone replaces his insect repellent with pig's blood. Have you seen Minnesota mosquitoes? They're horses with wings. It's like being bitten by a hornless unicorn.

But back to the marketing lounge.

Rod is introducing Chase, and I don't have to look to know that he's preening for his adoring fans. I can *smell* the estrogen his presence has prompted. Half of my coworkers just spontaneously ovulated.

6

So the guy could buy a small country. Who cares? He's also been known to pee in cornflakes.

Literally.

I didn't witness it, but my brothers told me later they didn't think I'd really eat the cereal.

Now the Dick is talking. I'd turn my headphones up, but Parker spilled her avocado mango acai berry chia energy smoothie on them last week and shorted something in the cord, which means One Direction sounds like they're being filtered through mashed bananas.

Yes, I like boy bands, and I'm not afraid to admit it. And I do a hell of a lot more than sing along, thank you very much.

"Morning, ladies and gentlemen." The Dick's voice is hot chocolate with a triple shot of espresso, and I hate myself for noticing. Why couldn't the smoothie filter *that* out? "Just wanted to stop in and say hi. Love what you've done here, and I'm excited to be a part of the Crunchy family."

I snort.

Family.

My brothers thought Chase was family once.

A chill washes over me, making my nipples tighten against my damp bra. Stupid boob sweat. Stupid racing heart. Stupid backstabbing billionaire.

Why did he get to be the one who grew up to become a billionaire?

"O.M.G. He's watching you." The message from Goth Parker adds a sour taste in my mouth to my already overactive physical impairments. My boob sweat is starting to stink.

When I don't reply, another message pops up. "You don't look good. Do you need an energy bar? Tell me you didn't go bar-hopping and have a one-night stand with Hottie McBillions last night. Oh, wait. Tell me you did. Then tell me everything else."

7

"Ah, Sia, always working hard." Rod raises his voice. "Sia? Sia! Tell Mr. Jett about the Choy Joy campaign."

Mr. Jett. Rod has twenty years on Chase, but since Chase has the fat bank account, it's *Mr. Jett.*

What would they call him if they knew what he did at the lake with my floaty toy that one summer? Hmm?

I pull off my headphones and mentally prepare myself for a public execution. I lever myself out of the beanbag chair—without stumbling, take *that*, Mr. Arms—and I turn, making myself stare straight into the pits of hell.

Or, you know, his eyes. Which are more of a Caribbean sea blue than cinder and ash. Deep-set under a prominent brow. Crackling and radiating with suppressed power. Erm, evil. Suppressed malevolence. Fire and brimstone. *What's that, Lassie? Ambrosia's better sense fell down the well?*

His eyes widen in horror before settling into a smarmy, wicked smirk that he probably practices in the mirror every night before swimming through his piles of money à la Scrooge McDuck.

Life is horrifically unfair sometimes.

But two can play the smirking game. I just happen to be saving mine for after I quit.

Or until after I convince him he's made a terrible investment and should immediately head to the nearest underground gambling hall to shed himself of this horrific burden. Or, you know, burden me with it instead.

Ambrosia Berger, CEO and owner of Crunchy. Nice ring to it. Could've happened, too, if he hadn't stolen my future from me. The bastard.

"The Choy Joy campaign is launching in three weeks across all our social media platforms," I tell the Dick. And I keep my voice pleasant and modulated as if I don't know he was the one responsible for what happened to my teddy bear in second grade. And lest you think all my grievances against him are from before puberty, believe me...They. Are. Not. "We're doing for bok choy what Beyoncé did for kale."

"Interesting." He strokes his chin, his index finger brushing over that dimple. I wonder if the lingering bits of his conscience are dried and shriveled enough that the motion dusts them out of their little hidey hole. "Your pairing suggestions?"

I rattle off a half-dozen quick meal ideas ranging from seafood to sweet potatoes.

"And sausages," he says.

Oh, no, he didn't.

"Sausages!" Madison squeals. "Oh, Mr. Jett, that's brilliant. Of course we'll add a recipe for Choy Joy Sausages."

Madison just said *Joy Sausages* in front of our new billionaire boss. Someday, I'll laugh at that. Today, however, is not that day.

"And bratwurst," Chase adds.

No.

He.

Did.

Not.

If I hadn't already seen the inside of a jail cell courtesy of this man—and a bratwurst, and no, I don't want to talk about it—I'd have my hands wrapped around his neck right now.

His smirk grows like he knows it. Damn him, that's the same smirk he wore last year on *People's* Sexiest Man of the Year cover. Which I only know because I work for a grocery store and we might be Crunchy, but *People* still sells, and I might've had that weird moment of realizing the man who took my virginity and crushed my soul was somehow the hottest rich man on the planet.

How often does that happen?

And because he's a dick, I couldn't even enjoy the moment.

"Definitely bratwurst." He nods to the group. "Appeal to sports fans."

Sports fans? Is he fucking kidding?

"We sell the best organic turkey bratwurst," Madison says.

Chase smiles at her. "Good to know, Ms...?"

"Madison." Her voice is breathy and her teeth are glowing like she's been overusing vegan tooth whitener again. "Madison O'Connor. The Joy Choy campaign was my idea."

"Was it now?" Chase's gaze slides to me. *A good boss would give credit where credit is due.* "I love it. Good work. Add the bratwurst."

For the love of Pete. If I'd told him it was her idea, he'd think I was throwing her under the bus. Or the Bratwurst Wagon.

Which I hadn't thought about in at least four months, jackass.

He waves like he's the king of fucking England. "Carry on. I look forward to working with each and every one of you."

Except you, Ambrosia May Berger.

The feeling is mutual, *Chases Tail* Jett.

Maybe I'll put off looking for that new job.

Last time, Chase won. He got my cherry, he got my pride, and he got to see me tossed in the slammer.

Now, his billions might stack the odds against me, but this is my home. My city. My job.

And this time, victory will be mine.

Chase Jett (The Dick)

AMBROSIA MAY BERGER.

Holy fucking shit.

Ten years, and she hasn't changed a bit. Tight body, perky breasts, wavy hair, luscious lips, *fuck me* written in every hot little glare.

I'd be happy to oblige her request, but there are a few things no amount of money can replace.

Like my dick if she slices it off.

And then there's my self-respect. It gets a vote in what my junk does these days. While I've had a hard time—*hard*, that's almost as good as *joy sausages*—with the joystick in my pants since I left the marketing department, my brain is kicking in with emergency killjoy procedures.

Which is why I've just excused myself from the Crunchy executives to take a private phone call, which couldn't have come at a better time.

"Hey." I kick back in my new chair and take in the view of

the city from my twentieth-floor office. "How's my favorite lady?"

"Chase! Honey, tell me you didn't buy a grocery store."

"Guilty as charged. You'll never have to pay for your organic, free-range chicken again." Not that I've been able to convince her to buy it in the last decade, but at least she's off canned baloney. "How's the Mediterranean?"

My mother rattles off all the things she's seen and done on this leg of her round-the-world tour. I count three inhales in five minutes, and I smile.

Good to hear her smile. She'd yelled at me for going overboard for her birthday present, but there's no one else I owe as much to.

Also, talking to my mother is killing this unwelcome hard-on.

And only partially because she's my mother. She's also the only other person in the world who fully understands the complication that is Ambrosia May Berger. Not that I'll ruin Mom's trip by mentioning Bro. Or *Sia* as she apparently goes by now.

See-uh. I don't like it. Doesn't fit her or sound anything like her real name. Makes her seem *city*-ish.

"What else are you buying while I'm gone?" Mom asks.

I extricate my dick from my brain and refocus. "I hear there's a whole town for sale in South Dakota," I tell her. "Big enough for a castle with a moat."

"Oh, stop." She laughs, but I know she'd love it. She always had a stack of romance novels that she borrowed from the library sitting by her bed. She also worked her ass off in the baloney factory for years to feed and clothe me. After everything my father put her through, she deserves an easy, carefree retirement.

I wasn't exactly innocent in the causes of her life difficulties either.

She blamed the Berger twins.

I like to think it's their sister's fault. Hell, I'd just liked to think about their sister *period*. Until she tried to throw me under the bus on the worst day of my life.

Bus. I snort dryly to myself. A bus would've been *normal*. But this was Ambrosia May Berger.

She went with *normal* like forks went with electrical outlets.

"We're docking in Mykonos next week for three days," Mom tells me.

Ah, the elusive *Mother Hint* peeks its head out. "Greece? Hmm. I suppose I could buy a country instead. I'll fly over and check it out. How's Tuesday?"

She laughs again. "Oh, honey, you'd have to be a trillionaire to buy Greece."

"Challenge accepted."

This is what matters. Family. Home. Good food. And buying small countries.

Not Ambrosia May Berger.

Ambrosia

THE BASTARD SENT bratwurst to the entire building for lunch.

I saved mine. I cut it up in little pieces, tossed the carnage in one of the glass storage jars Crunchy provides for employees to borrow in an effort to save the world, and took it home.

Tomorrow I'll come to my senses and realize that just because Chase Jett once hid raw chicken gizzards in my dollhouse and is now taunting me with the lowest moment of my life doesn't mean I should break into his Upper East Side brownstone and hide decaying chunks of bratwurst in his curtain rods.

Yes, I Googled him and I know where he lives. It's not stalking. Just wanted to make sure we wouldn't be on the same subway home or shopping at the same neighborhood Crunchy.

My upstairs neighbors are at it again. *Squeaky-squeaky-squeeeeeeeak.*

"Woo pig sooie," I call to the ceiling.

Hogzilla's mating squeal is my answer.

I feed Dolphin, my goldfish, and water Gabby, my aloe plant on the fire escape, before grabbing my keyboard for band practice. I might be headed for the unemployment office tomorrow, but that's no excuse to miss rehearsals. A girl needs a career backup plan.

Parker and I play in a boy band cover band at a bar on 23rd and 7th most Saturday nights. Okay, fine. It's a juice bar, but that's by choice. Anyway, Parker has mad guitar skills. I can carry a tune and plunk out a little more than *Chopsticks*.

We picked up Eloise at a yoga class. None of us know what she does for her day job, but she can bang the hell out of a set of drums. Willow is our lead vocalist. She does an uncanny Justin Timberlake, and I don't care what those other boy band cover bands offer her—or if her stepfather, who's literally the king of a tiny Viking nation, ever demands that she leave New York to move to her step-home country—I will fight to the death to keep her.

She's *ours*. Don't even think about it, man. I will cut you. With my mad sarcasm skills, because that's pretty much all I have after the great knife-and-superglue incident in high school—*thanks again, Chase Jett*—but you get the point.

I arrive at Parker's building and head to the basement, but my three musicians-in-crime aren't set up to practice.

Unless you use the word *practice* lightly, in which case we might be preparing for Oktoberfest. In May. With whisky.

I take one look at the three of them huddled around a bottle of Crown in the middle of the laundry room, and my chest squeezes. "Hey, guys. What's up?"

It's Willow, I'm certain. She's a slender, sparkly-eyed, dark-haired optimist engaged to a socially- and royally-acceptable day trader who works too much and has too many cats. If he weren't the sweetest man on the entire planet—weird for a day-trading cat lover, I know, but it's Martin—we might've staged an intervention long before he gave her a ring, and not just because it took him seven years to propose. Still, wedding planning has been something akin to mud wrestling a giraffe in a lava pit, and only partially because she's having the wedding in her stepfather's kingdom.

They turn as one to glare at me, and I realize it's not Willow and her wedding plans prompting the alcohol. Nor is Eloise having issues with a new boyfriend, nor is Parker freaking out that she's going to be fired.

Parker gives me the wide-eyeball *I am furious with you sit down right now you have so much explaining to do can I borrow that dress I* LOVE *it* finger point of doom. "*Sit.*"

"You're not from Philadelphia," Willow says.

"Pittsburgh," Eloise corrects.

See? No one can keep those Pennsylvania P-cities straight. Or spell *Pennsylvania* right the first time. It's the perfect cover. Or, it was until today.

Thanks, Google. And thanks, grocery store-buying Dick.

"There either." Parker shoves her phone in my face, and before I can make out the teensy-tiny words—I get the joy of a challenge, but I think she could've picked a better character-building challenge than tiny-print-reading—the shrieking starts.

"*You were arrested naked in the Bratwurst Wagon in Hottie McBillionaire's Minnesota hometown!*" is basically the gist of it.

And it's all true.

Also, incomplete, but I don't think my friends will appreciate that at the moment.

"Did you know him?" Willow demands.

"More important, did you sleep with him?" Eloise has this

three-pack-a-day voice that she says runs in her mother's family, and she carries a lighter because it's easier than repeating *Sorry, I don't smoke* fourteen times a day.

"Shut *up*." Parker's getting more shrill than Willow when she does her Jordan Knight impersonation. "Friends tell each other things. *Things like this*."

I reach for the Crown and take a hit straight from the bottle. "Yes, yes, and I'm only sorry I got caught," I reply in answer to their questions.

Parker sucks in a horrified breath.

Eloise perks up though. "Go on."

"Can I keep this?" I wave the bottle at them.

"*In Royal Veritas*," Willow says.

My mother was a Greek philosophy professor at the University of Minnesota extension down the road—if you think Ambrosia May is bad, my twin brothers are Zeus November and Ares February. While I could pick a Greek god out of a lineup, Latin is lost on me.

"*In Crown Royal, there is truth*," Eloise translates. "And we want the *whole* truth."

Outside of work hours, my band is my family. If I could've had sisters, I would've picked these three. Given my brothers, picking sisters was safer than leaving it to the luck of the freakish genetic combinations my parents were capable of making. But the point is, I know about Eloise's sixth toe, Willow's fear of butterflies, and Parker's obsession with Tarzan.

We're as tight as if we're actually blood sisters, and I owe them the truth.

"Yes, I was arrested for grand theft Bratwurst Wagon when I was eighteen," I confess to their expectant faces.

"That is so fucking cool," Eloise whispers in her deep rasp.

"My little *stunt*, as my parents called it, got me expelled from Vassar before I even started."

I glug off the bottle again while the three of them wince together. I love my job, I love living in the city, I love my friends, but Vassar would've been the difference between low-level management at a small-organic-potatoes grocery store and a full marketing gig at Whole Foods.

"The naked part?" Eloise prompts.

"Ritualistic virginity shedding with my brothers' best friend." I go for a casual shrug and miss the mark by my whole body. It wasn't casual then. It was—I don't know what it was.

Fierce. Angry. Competitive.

Un-fucking-believably hot. Dirty. Wicked.

Double-orgasmic.

Transcendent.

And just plain *wrong*.

"Doesn't everyone want to do it in the Bratwurst Wagon?" I ask to their slack-jawed response.

"Must be a Minnesota thing," Parker says darkly.

I obviously have some work to do to get off my friends' shit lists. Crown Royal, give me strength.

"I didn't plan it." I grab my phone and open the Dick List. Right there on top is his name. *Chase. Dick Number One.* Parker's added two dicks to the list. Eloise has seven. Willow doesn't like to call people dicks, so we added her landlord and three stepbrothers for her. "Once he hid all my Barbies' clothes and told me they were prostitutes damned to Hell. I was, like, seven. He ripped every other page out of my copy of *The Secret Garden*. Every time he'd come over, he'd be like, *Hey, Bro, got something for you* and then he'd pull a dead mosquito out of his pocket and hand it to me one wing and leg at a time. And that was all *before* puberty."

"He sounds disturbed," Willow murmurs.

My mom had told me once that we didn't know what went on behind closed doors, and we should all be thankful that a boy like Chase had such good influences as my brothers.

That should tell you something right there.

Or she had a momentary lapse in reality. These were the same brothers who had convinced me that I'd die if I didn't eat a teaspoon of boogers every day *and who donated to the cause.*

"I don't know what his deal was, but when he gave me a case of canned baloney for my twelfth birthday, I was done. I started pranking him back. After six years of war, the Bratwurst Wagon came to town for the baloney festival, and I knew if I didn't do something first, he would. I was going to leave a trail of sausages from the Bratwurst Wagon to his house, but he was already there, armed with spray paint."

"I think I see where this is going," Eloise says.

"The two of us breaking into the Bratwurst Wagon, having mad angry sex on the floor under the sausages, and then trying to Bonnie and Clyde our way out of trouble? Yeah, that pretty much sums it up."

As much as I wanted to relive out loud anyway.

Hey, Bro. I can't decide if I should draw a picture of you, or if I should just write Bro Likes To Eat Me *on this giant wrinkled sausage,* he'd said when I'd caught him with the spray paint.

I'd told him to fuck off. He'd told me to fuck him. I'd said he couldn't handle me. He'd said I should put my mouth where his dick was.

And somehow we'd discovered the Bratwurst Wagon was open, with the keys in the ignition, and flinging insults at each other was weirdly erotic, and then we'd gone at each other like—well, like my upstairs neighbors, though I prefer to think I was more lioness than Miss Piggy.

I'd felt supercharged. Electrified. More alive than alive.

And somewhere in the hazy midst of lust and fury, right between me telling him he had a crooked dick and him shoving it so deep inside me I couldn't tell where he ended and I began—or if he'd get stuck in there, I was a virgin, I didn't know—I saw the oddest craving in his eyes.

Like he wanted to stay there. With me. All night.

Say something nice. Lick a soft trail up my neck instead of sinking his teeth into my tender skin. Trace his name on my belly.

His barriers had gone up so fast I was sure I'd imagined it, but what if I hadn't?

And that's when the flash of red and blue lights had come through the front window of the Bratwurst Wagon.

"He wasn't mentioned in the article we found on you," Parker says.

"We saw the lights, he said *Go*, and while I went for the keys, he went for the back door."

Willow sucks in a grin. "That's a rather impressive misunderstanding."

"Or one hell of a setup."

"Aw, Sia, you really think he set you up?"

"I told the cops he was with me, but he denied everything. Which left me the crazy naked chick leading the police on a thirty-mile-an-hour Bratwurst Wagon chase around Wishberry Lake at two in the morning."

Parker's nose is flaring, lips twitching. Willow's not even trying to suppress her laughter. And yeah—ten years later, I can see how it might be funny to someone who didn't end up sleeping on a concrete jail floor and then pled guilty to public indecency and destruction of property to get the grand theft auto charge dropped, only to get a phone call rescinding my enrollment to my dream college while being crowned the new laughingstock of my hometown. The hometown I still haven't been back to.

My family comes to me for the holidays. They don't even ask me to go home.

Maybe it's still not funny.

Only Eloise isn't laughing. "How does a guy go from being a grade-A dick to a billionaire buying out organic grocery stores?" she asks.

"Don't know, don't care." I take another swig of whisky.

"You remember when *Frenemy Crush* was huge on Facebook?" Parker asks.

Cold dread washes over me. "That matching game that uses your six least favorite Facebook friends' profile pictures for game pieces that you explode with flaming darts and volcanic blasts?" I whisper.

"Yeah, that one."

"I fucking loved that game," Eloise growls.

"At my mom's wedding, I saw the princes playing it using the profile pictures of the heads of other countries," Willow says.

"Mr. Jett built it," Parker tells us.

"The Dick," I correct.

"The Dick." She nods. "Anyway, he made a killing on the game, invested his profits in some tech startups that paid off big-time, and now he's diversifying. Healthcare, energy, transportation. He even owns a small publishing company."

"Great. All he needs is a construction company and a bank and he can buy his own town and the friends to put in it."

"I wouldn't move there," Willow says.

Eloise smiles darkly. "I would, but only to poison the water supply."

Have I mentioned my undying love for Eloise? And that's not the alcohol talking. "Anyway, the good news is, I'll have way more time to practice my keyboard skills soon."

"What? Why?" Parker asks.

21

"My current moral dilemma. Refuse to let Chase Jett's presence in my workplace affect me and do my job anyway like a big girl, or quit because I refuse to let him boss me around while he profits off my work? And let's not forget to take into account the increased probability that I'll be terminated because of our history."

"If he fires you because he banged you and left you in the Bratwurst Wagon, you can sue him for wrongful termination," Willow offers.

I almost smile. Willow said *banged*.

"But if she decorates his office with dicks and sends a company-wide exposé memo, he'll almost have to fire her, and *then* she can call in the lawyers." Eloise for the win, ladies and gentleman.

"Being fired wouldn't be all terrible." I hiccup. "Maybe I'll be a subway performer. I could start writing original songs. *I went to jail for banging a billionaire in the Bratwurst Wagon* has a ring to it, don't you think?"

And to think, I've wasted a decade of my life being mortified by my youthful discretion. I'd level up in cool points with at least half the marketing department if they knew.

"Uh-oh," Parker says.

"What?"

"Anti-dick moves. According to Wikipedia, he runs in the St. Jude Marathon every year. Also, since officially reaching billionaire status two years ago, he's built a new no-kill shelter in upstate Minnesota and started a foundation that's running food banks in four states."

"If I had a billion dollars, I could buy a PR company and look like an angel too." Eloise taps a drumstick against her thigh. "You know what you need to do, don't you?"

"Legally change my name and apply to be a maid at Willow's stepdad's place? They need fresh, young, non-incestuous blood to bear a few royal babies, don't they?"

Willow goes pink. "I don't think my stepbrothers have any issues finding non-incestuous blood."

"You need to sleep with him again," Eloise declares.

I've mentioned how much I hate Eloise, haven't I?

She pushes her cats-eye glasses back up her nose. "You're lacking in closure."

"The only *closure* I need is to not work for the man who let me take the fall for our Bratwurst Wagon adventure. Either he goes or I go."

Eloise taps her drumstick again. "Do you *want* to go?"

"Um, *no*."

"Then we need a plan. He might have a billion dollars, but we have something he doesn't."

All three of us stare at her blankly.

"The collective outrage of scorned women everywhere," she says as though it should be obvious.

"Uh, sure," Parker says.

"We owe it to women everywhere to show this pompous prick that we're done doing jail time for his crimes while he rakes in the dough."

"I'd rather just forget it ever happened," I say. And honestly? I would. All of it. I've moved on. He's moved on. My brothers have moved on.

The Bratwurst Wagon has moved on.

Maybe in another ten or twenty years, I'll even be able to go home again.

"But I'd feel happier staying at Crunchy if he agreed to donate fifty percent of his profits to charity every year. That's reasonable, right? Then I'm not working for *him*. I'm working for charity."

"Charity?" Eloise snorts. "No, the man has to pay, and we're just the women to make him do it. We collectively have ten brothers. If anyone can find ways to torture a man, we can."

"Um, can we not count mine?" Willow says. "I don't know them all that well."

"That's okay. Mine count for three apiece," I tell her.

"That's eleven brothers then." Eloise smiles. "We're going to hand this dick his balls."

4

Chase

INDESCRIBABLE AS IT is for a kid who grew up wrong side of the lake in a little Minnesota town to own a thirty-million-dollar brownstone overlooking Central Park on the Upper East Side, something about the townhouse makes me claustrophobic. Maybe it's the hemmed-in feel of sharing walls with the neighbors on all seven floors. Maybe it's the dark tones of all the furniture, natural woodwork, and modern art.

Or maybe it's the faint smell of cigar lingering like a ghost.

Whatever it is, I decide I prefer the office at 3 AM. I own several—offices in New York, that is—but tonight I'm drawn back to Crunchy.

Best part of owning a grocery store—unlimited midnight snack options. Maybe I'll buy a condom company next.

On second thought, that's like buying a sports car. Looks like you're compensating.

The security guards on the first floor leap to their feet when I walk in. You wouldn't know it from the outside, but this building is worth its weight in gold. Crunchy's more than your standard organic grocery store.

It's also a successful experiment in growing food in the city. There are six floors of vegetables planted, tended, harvested, packaged, and shipped out to our local stores here every day. Security is non-negotiable.

I nod to the guards. "Evening, gentlemen. How's night watch?"

They share a look. "Good," the first says while the second trips over himself to get out, "All quiet and normal, sir."

I didn't squander my youth being a hellion to not see through the lies. I could fire them on the spot, but that kind of power isn't my thing.

I'd rather get the rush of the game before I decide their fate. "Excellent. Carry on."

The building is quiet tonight, except for a hiccup echoing down the hall.

Odd.

Even odder, and most unwelcome?

Ambrosia May Berger is standing in the elevator bank, peering up at the numbers. She hiccups again. I stop beside her and watch her eyes go wide, then narrow, then cross. Mirrored elevator doors are possibly the second greatest invention known to man.

First, of course, is the internet.

I stare at Bro in the door mirror.

She stares back.

For all the shit she gave me growing up, I always respected her spine. As much as one *can* respect something that infuriating. She got away with everything. Even when she was reckless.

I can honestly say no woman I've been with since her has ever tried to make a break for it in the Bratwurst Wagon.

As long as I block out the month that followed, I can think of the Bratwurst Wagon with a smile.

"Working late or coming in early?" I ask.

"The hogs are mating again," she replies.

The world believes this woman to be a sane, competent adult. Mind-boggling.

"Do you always wait in elevator banks for women you want to harass?" she asks.

"Only when I've gotten bored staking out the bathrooms." I reach over and hit the *up* button, because she hasn't. "Do you always assume the elevators can read your mind?"

"They were doing better than you. I didn't want to go up."

"And you're standing here because...?"

"It's my thinking spot."

"It's 3 AM on a Wednesday morning."

"Do you see me judging you on wanting to use an elevator at 3 AM on a Wednesday morning? No, you don't. So why do you have to judge me for wanting to think in an elevator bank at 3 AM? Hmmmmmmm?" The hum trills up on the end, right in time with her swiveling to face me. She squints one eye, then the other, before scrunching her face, pointing her index finger at my nose, and making *pew, pew* noises.

If *this* is what the security guards were worried I'd find, I'm rather disappointed.

"Drinking on the job again?" I ask.

"*Again* implies I've done it before. Which I have not, unless you count that time the guava kale juice fermented, which I don't, because it only counts as drinking if I enjoy the alcohol. Also, all whisky was consumed off-premise."

"So you're drunk."

"I'm not *drunk*. I'm barely buzzed enough to be able to tolerate you."

I eye her and decide she's telling the truth. Her eyes are too focused and her tongue's too sharp for her to be drunk. I can't even smell anything on her. Tired, maybe, but not drunk.

"Was it organic?" I ask dryly.

"It's whisky, dickhead."

Christ, that mouth. I want to lick it and tape it shut all at the same time. "You shouldn't call your superiors names."

She blows a raspberry. The sight of her ripe pink tongue makes my cock leap to attention.

"Looking for disciplinary action?" I murmur.

"Oh, don't you wish." The elevator dings, and she lists inside. I'd try to catch her, but frankly, I wouldn't mind seeing her crash to the ground.

She comes to a solid stop at the railing along the back paneled wall. "And you're not my superior," she says.

"I write your paycheck."

"Not yet you haven't." Spittle shouldn't be sexy, but her second raspberry gives me a longer look at her tongue. I remember that tongue. Long as a lizard's, hot as a volcano, talented as a porn star.

That's as complimentary as I get where Bro Berger is concerned.

"So Mr. Liver-bellied Bratwurst-runner-away-er," she says, "wouldn't you be happier owning a grocery store that I don't work for? Because I'm sure we can find another zagillionaire to take your place."

I punch the button to the eighteenth floor—where the fresh greens for tomorrow are being picked and packed right now, if all's on schedule—and give her my worst smile. "Aw, Bro, your inflated opinion of my bank account is touching."

"You could be a mega-ka-billion-trillionaire, and you still wouldn't have enough money to buy a soul."

I'm relatively new to the ranks of the ten-figure club, but it's still been years since anyone has insulted me to my face.

Her blatant hatred is oddly erotic. "Who needs a soul when I have the power to sack tempestuous employees?"

"Go ahead. I dare you." She bangs the button for the fourth floor. Then the third, fifth, seventh, ninth, and every odd number to the top. With a frown, she draws her hand down the row of even numbers until every single floor is lit, and if I'd still thought this was alcohol motivating her, the sharp, devious intention in her cold eyes removes any doubt.

She's fully in control and she's intentionally trying to bait me.

Heat creeps over my scalp. It's working.

She's making this elevator stop on Every. Single. Fucking. Floor.

I whip out my cell phone—security can override her little prank—but as the doors close, my signal dies.

She does the MC Hammer dance, and her breasts jiggle under her swishy spring dress in a way even a celibate Tibetan monk couldn't resist. There's no fucking way she's wearing a bra.

My cock twitches harder.

How did a woman so insanely evil land the world's most perfect tits?

"Go on, rich boy." She switches to the Lawnmower, and now her hips are rocking it too. "Buy your way out of *that*."

Good Chase, the businessman, the gaming tech genius, the face I show the world, the smarter part of my brain, hops off when the doors open on the second floor, because he appreciates stairs and getting the hell away from this deranged woman.

Bad Chase, though, has possessed my body and keeps me in the elevator.

I wave goodbye to rational thought and better judgment —who needs those bitches anyway?—and turn to Bro with a growl.

She's wiggling her sweet curvy ass at me now, arms circling, stirring the batter. *"It's my birthday, happy birthday, it's my birth—oomph!"*

Huh. Emergency stop button works, but it's a little choppy on the execution. Better have maintenance look at that tomorrow.

I take one large, purposeful step toward Bro.

She fists her hands on her hips and calls me an asshole with her dark, heavy-lidded, fuck-me bedroom eyes.

Yeah.

She's feeling it too.

That pull. That hate. That inexplicable force of rage that can only be satiated with a hard, hot fuck.

"I fucking hate bok choy," I growl.

"Then you shouldn't have bought a fucking organic grocery store," she growls back in a perfect mockery of me.

I've always detested her ability to do that. I take another step, and we're toe-to-toe. The lead pipe in my pants is poking her belly. My sanity has fled the building. Maybe the whole city. Hell, it's just skyrocketed out of the fucking atmosphere.

This woman drives me mad. She's obnoxious as toe fungus and pathologically self-righteous. I want to crush her. I want to ruin her. I want to *own* her.

"Not enough bratwurst for one day?" she hisses. "You had to put a crooked one in your pocket too?" Her eyes are obsidian ringed in gold, pillowy lips parted, her hands fisted in my sweatshirt.

I back her into the corner, my dick doing all the talking. "You want my long, thick cock, and you know it."

"I want to break it in two and feed it to maggots."

"You want to bite it. And suck on it. And ride it."

"I fucking hate you."

I fucking hate her too, but I have a fistful of her hair, and I'm suddenly doing the only thing I know to do to shut her the fuck up.

I'm shoving my tongue down her throat. As far as it'll go. Gliding into that hot, wet, silky mouth where my joystick wants to be.

She sinks her nails into my ass and yanks me tighter against her, matching me thrust for thrust with her lizard tongue while she grunts incoherent insults.

I jerk my hips against her, rubbing my cock against her tight body. *That's for costing me my two best friends.*

She wraps her long giraffe legs around my hips and rides me like she doesn't know how to stay on the bull. I twist and shove her against the back wall, yank her skirt up, and dry-hump her like a freak. She's drenched, soaking through her thong and coating my pants.

I take my tongue out of her mouth and bite her shoulder. She rakes her claws up my back under my shirt. "You are such an asshole," she says.

"Save it for someone who cares, Bro."

She bucks harder against me, and I silence her again, diving into her mouth like I'd like to dive into her pussy.

Licking. Sucking. Eating.

Mine. Mine to command. Mine to conquer. Mine to ruin for life.

Because she'll *never* get dick like I can give. No one else knows her. They don't know her dark side. Her evil side. Her carnal side.

I slide a finger under her panties and run it over her

smooth seam. She moans in my mouth and rides my hand, twisting, demanding, as if she thinks she can give the orders.

In her dreams.

I pull my hand away.

"That's right, fucker," she hisses. "You can't handle my pussy."

I shove my hand between us again, and this time, I go straight for the kill. Thumb to her clit, all four fingers sliding up into her creamy channel.

She comes so hard, clenching around me so tight, I feel every spasm all the way to my elbow. Head thrown back, legs straight out, eyes rolling out of her head like a camel having a seizure while she rides my hand through the waves. Her high-pitched cry, "You *diiiiiiiiiick*," echoes in the elevator, and the room wobbles in the shaft.

That's right, Bro.

Zero to sixty in four-point-three seconds. Good luck getting that with one of your crunchy, free-range, organic toadstool boyfriends.

And we haven't even gotten to the main event.

I consider dropping her on her ass while she's a pile of rotten jelly in my arms, but instead wait until her eyes focus again. Fucking gentleman of the year, that's me.

When she blinks at me, I give her another moment to remember she hates me. It's remarkable, watching the transformation. One minute, she almost looks human, and the next she's a screaming harpy with horns and vampire teeth.

"Two-point-one," she says.

"Seconds to make you come?" I breathe. "You're easy."

"I didn't come," she lies. "That was my body recoiling in horror, and you get a two-point-one a scale of zero to one hundred."

I chuckle. "We both know better, Bro. Now suck my dick."

"Suck your own dick."

I suck her juices off my fingers, and her breathing goes shallow. She licks her lips, and her greedy hands plunge into my pants to grab my aching cock.

I know she's trying to strangle it, but sweet *Christ*, there's pain, and then there's pleasure, and fuck if I'll let her know she's mastered the art of riding that line.

With superhuman strength, I force myself to affect a bored eye roll. "Oh. Ow. Stop. That hurts." I give enough of a thrust in her grip to tell her if she stops, I'll fucking jack myself off in front of her, and she squeezes harder.

Fuck, that's good.

Her fist yanks me like she's a virgin milkmaid, and I'm blinded by a white-hot streak of furious lust. I'm enraged. I'm engorged. I'm—

She grabs me by the balls, scraping my sack, and that color behind my eyeballs goes iridescent. Beyond white. I can't think. I can't talk. I can barely keep my knees from giving out.

"Flaccid," she whispers. "And still crooked. You should see a doctor about that."

"If you don't like it, you could quit touching it." If she quits touching me, I'm going to fucking die. "I can barely tell your hand is there anyway."

"It's a mercy stroke. I'm generous like that. And you're a lying fuck-face."

"Beg all you want. I'm not giving you a pity fuck."

"I don't want a pity fuck. It's all I can do to not barf while I'm looking at you."

I pry my eyelids open, and see by the way her eyes have gone round that we're thinking the same thing.

I'm picturing her ass in the air, those two perfect globes in my hands while my dick fills and stretches her hot, weeping pussy, and I almost come all over her dress. She still has a handful of my balls, an iron grip on my cock, and I'm so fucking turned on I might blow a new hole out of my nut sack.

This woman does abnormal, not-right things to my brain. And my body. And my mouth.

"Bend over, cabbage face," I order.

"Why? You couldn't find my g-spot with a flashlight and a guide."

"Fine. Look me in the eye while I go spelunking." I finger the strap of her thong, thrusting into her grip on my cock, praying this is a bad dream.

"I really fucking hate you." She tosses her dress over her head, and *oh sweet Christ in a pickup truck*, all she's wearing is the thong. Her cherry nipples point to high heaven, her waist curves into sweet honey hips, and all that's between me and the promised land is a strip of black lace.

If she were any other woman, I'd bite that off her and spend the next two hours with my face buried between her legs.

But this is Bro, and I will *not* shoot my shit before I'm buried in her pussy or I'll never fucking live this down, so I grab with both hands and split the lace in two.

And—god help me—she's bare as a hairless cat.

Before I can inspect further, she has her head in the corner, ass in the air, and I'm fumbling—fucking *fumbling*—to remember what to do with my dick. I lean over and bite one cheek. She shudders and wiggles her ass.

"Knew you couldn't find—"

Her last word is lost in a gasp as I dive into that slick, pink home between her thighs and keep gliding until my balls slap her skin. And then I pump. And thrust. I grab her hips and gyrate, filling her, taking her, riding her, owning her, over and over and over.

She's wet and tight and everything a woman should be

and nothing Bro should be, because this isn't *sex*. This is a game. This is power. This is about winning. About showing her she's *nothing* to me. About getting off. And I'm almost there. One more thrust, one more—

She arches her back and thrusts her ass into me until she's squishing my tight balls, the spasms coming hot and fast and glorious around my dick, and I'm done. I come like I've never come in my life. Not the night I lost my virginity, not the night she pissed me off so bad we hate-fucked in the ride-on bratwurst, not with any of the actresses or musicians who've wanted to bang a billionaire.

And I keep coming. She keeps coming. It's one endless orgasm, her clenching around me, me spilling everything I have until I'm pretty sure I'm coming blood.

Or at least brain cells.

Because *why the fuck am I fucking Bro Berger in a fucking elevator at three in the morning?*

I jerk back and yank my pants up. She melts to the floor, panting, and that's when I realize my second mistake.

We didn't use a condom.

We didn't fucking use a condom.

"Get up," I order.

She's still breathing heavy, knees spread wide, hand to her heart, but she spares a minute to flip me off.

"Fucking *get up*," I say. "Why didn't you have a fucking condom?"

Her body stills. Slowly, so slowly I'm not sure she's moving, she lifts her head to look at me. She doesn't say anything. She doesn't have to. It's written all over her face.

Checkmate.

Delicately covering her breasts, she slides her legs around as if she can find some modesty now. She lifts her head to the ceiling, blows a kiss and a smirk to the round black orb that

35

tells me *the fucking security guards are watching*, and the elevator jerks to life again.

Her dress is still falling to cover her ass as she steps off the elevator on the third floor. "Better luck next time, Jett. Keep the panties. Last souvenir you'll ever have."

I'm a billionaire, and I've just been schooled by a woman who once stole the Bratwurst Wagon.

I'm fucked.

5

Ambrosia

OH. My. God.

First things first—I'm on the pill. I *absolutely* would've preferred the Dick use a condom, but after everything he's put me through in my life, I'm not going to feel bad if he gets a few nights of lost sleep over the idea of me having his demon spawn. I'll tell him in a day or two. When I'm over the fact that his cooties are currently leaking out my vagina and that tonight could've turned into the title of a romance novel. *Having My Dickhead Billionaire Boss's Baby.*

Thank *god* for the pill.

Second—

"When I said *distract the guards*, I didn't mean *have sex with Chase Jett*," Parker whisper-shrieks when I meet back up with her and Eloise in an all-night coffee shop two blocks behind the office.

"What? It's not like I *enjoyed* it," I lie. Oh my holy *god*, I suddenly don't know why Hogzilla over my apartment even bothers with the squeaky bedsprings. She could be having elevator sex. With a billionaire whose crooked dick grew three inches since the last time I saw it. Are penis extensions a real thing? Because if I were a dude with a billion dollars, and it didn't hurt, I'd totally go for that. And I swear to god, if he ever gets that curve in it straightened out, I'll kill him, because the things that curve did to my—

Ah, because it's *obviously* a serious issue, and I like knowing Chase Jett's penis is malformed. My nipples aren't still hard and turned on. Your nipples are hard. Shut up.

Parker snaps her fingers in front of my face. "You *didn't* enjoy it?"

Yeah, I don't believe me either. "Not on purpose."

"If you have to have sex, might as well be good sex," Eloise says.

Word. I'm never taking off my pants for anything less than a double-orgasm event again.

"Did you get into his office?" I ask.

That's the important part. And it shouldn't be this difficult to concentrate on remembering why I was in the building in the first place.

Parker's right. I was supposed to be the distraction. And I did a damn good job, didn't I?

Eloise smiles. She has a truly terrifying smile. "In and out and completely unspotted. He'll be cleaning glitter out of his butt crack and fingernails for the next year." She gives me a fist bump, which I return despite the regrets seeping in.

I hadn't been sober enough to object to Eloise's idea of leaving Chase a present in his office when we left band practice, but I also wasn't drunk enough to blame the elevator on the alcohol.

Who knew we'd hit a double header? Not the orgasms—which should be illegal and horrifying and not so explosive that I can still feel my vagina trembling and asking for *more please* because *Chase Jett is a dickhead*. A dickhead with a magic bent penis and fingers that can—

Double header.

Right.

The *vengeance* double header. Parker and Eloise set up glitter bombs in Chase's office while I had exhibitionist revenge elevator sex with him while the security guards watched. And to think, I thought I'd be keeping their attention by sneaking around the employee snack bar.

"Do your security cameras record footage, or just run a live stream?" Eloise asks.

My heart stops.

Like, literally stops. Because I don't know the answer to that, but I do know—

"Benny," Parker whispers. She's gone even paler than me, and I'm from Minnesota. She shakes my shoulders. "Sia, he's sleeping with Tisha in accounting."

Eloise gives the universal *Go on, say something that makes sense* gesture.

I grab the canvas sack Parker was using to carry her and Eloise's disguises and wish it was a brown paper sack, because breathing into organic, fair trade cotton isn't helping. And it's not because I have a weird thing about the lion mask staring up at me with empty black eyes.

"Benny's one of the night guards." Parker's voice is barely audible over my heaving. "Tisha's the reason Crunchy had to issue a gossip policy. The whole company's going to know about this by morning."

Enter Chase Jett.

Exit my normal life.

Again.

6

Ambrosia

I REFUSE to hide behind my shame or regrets, so I'm at the office at the bright and early hour of 10 AM, hopped up on fair trade, organic caramel soy lattes and ready to talk our internally-grown bok choy.

Unfortunately, I barely make it in the door before I'm summoned to the executive floor.

Once I finished hyperventilating and got a shower in the wee hours of the morning, Eloise and Parker and I huddled together in my apartment, blasting Taylor Swift to cover Hogzilla's squeaky bedsprings while we discussed the best way to handle the aftermath of my sexual nuclear explosion, and then we all went home for naps before work.

I'm ready. I can do this.

I hold my head high and take the elevator as if Chase and I hadn't banged each other's brains out in it last night. I try to hold my breath, because if I can still smell us in there, I might lose it.

When the doors slide open on the executive floor, even the potted plants turn to each other and whisper.

I can forgive the plants. I mean, what else do they have to do all day besides sit around, look green, and hope housekeeping remembers to water them?

But the random execs and sub-execs and secretaries who are all looking at me like I need to wear a scarlet whore letter the rest of my days damn well better be thinking Chase Jett needs a matching one.

Rod Xavier steps out of his office and crooks a finger at me before my heels hit the organic, fair trade, sustainably-harvested bamboo-and-corn silk rug in the lobby. He looks as though someone has plucked all the cherry tomatoes off his bushes a week before they would've been ripe and used them to spell *Ambrosia has a big penis* in his parents' driveway.

Bad metaphor. Sorry. I'm still scarred from that memory, okay?

Inside Rod's office, all the seats save the interrogation chair are occupied. I take stock of the suits in the room—joining Rod are Crunchy's president, vice president, head of HR, and the chief of security.

Usually the only time I see these guys together is on the picture wall in the downstairs lobby.

They're all smiling in the lobby.

Not so much here.

"Ambrosia, have a seat," Rod says.

Not a chance. I'll go down standing, thank you very much. "What's this about?" I ask with a sweet smile. Eloise's idea. She says men love the sweet smile. It lulls them into a false sense of security.

Right now, it's making half of them shift like they're trying to hide untimely flatulence, and the other half have assumed the *very disappointed in you* Dad Frown.

"Ambrosia, you were seen in the building at three AM this morning," Rod says.

I continue to smile my bland, innocent smile.

"In the elevator," he clarifies.

Don't blush, Sia. Don't blush. "Mm."

"Without..." Rod pauses to gulp his coffee and wipe his brow. "Without your clothes on," he finishes.

"Was I?" I ask.

"Very much so," the chief of security says, as though he's seen the video.

"Mm," I repeat. Because what else does one say in this kind of situation?

"Sia." Rod strokes his mustache. "We have certain expectations of our employees, clearly spelled out in the employee handbook—"

"And I'm glad we do," I interrupt. "The gossip has really become a problem lately, and it's interfering with office morale and productivity. By the way, has Mr. Jett received a copy of the employee handbook?"

The president is eyeballing me like I'm an overripe, pesticide-ridden apple grown over a landfill. The head of security's bald head is so red, I wonder if embarrassment alone could fry a free-range egg. And Rod—who was praising my team just yesterday—seems to want to sink through the floor.

"You were observed on video engaging in sexual activities in the workplace," Rod says gently. "We're going to have to let you go."

I keep smiling even though my heart is hammering chips off my lungs. "Is Mr. Jett being let go?"

"Sia, Mr. Jett *owns* the company."

"You're saying that because I was observed in a closed room, just me and the owner of the company and however many security guards were glued to their monitors watching us while other suspicious characters were roaming the hallways, and Mr. Jett appeared to be taking liberties with my more personal body parts, that he gets to stay and I have to leave?"

A stony silence meets my question.

"I'm going to have to decline being let go," I announce. "And I'm afraid I'm going to have to call my lawyers. And my state representatives. Definitely a few celebrity gossip sites. Mr. Jett *is* technically a celebrity, so they'll want to know. Stuff like this spreads over social media like wildfire. I mean, I hate the hit that Crunchy will take, considering our core customer demographic is seventy-percent women between the ages of twenty-six and forty who are politically active and socially conscious, many of whom have daughters, but it's hard to see how you could possibly let me keep my job and take a stand for women's sexual liberation and the accountability of man. I mean, your security guards saw my boobs. Federal offense right there."

I finally take the seat they've offered, because if I don't, my knees are going to give out. "Or," I say, "you can call Mr. Jett in here, and we can work out an amenable arrangement for all of us."

Dots are dancing in front of my eyes. I wonder if there are any nunneries hiring in the city. Being a nun sounds damn good right now. Except for the part where I'll probably have to quit saying *damn*.

"We're prepared to give you a very generous severance package and a glowing letter of recommendation," Rod says.

What? *What?* Were they even listening to me? Crap. Where am I going to find a lawyer who can take on Chase and his billions? Between the Bratwurst Wagon incident and now this—which I'm *certain* will be leaked to celebrity gossip sites imminently if they fire me, *because I'll fucking tell them myself*—my chances of finding a comparable new job are next to zero.

Which means the only thing I have left is my pride. I shove out of the seat, fury once again the main ingredient fueling my veins. "Gentlemen, you can take your crunchy, orgasmic food and shove it up all your collective, sexist asses."

I spin toward the door, and—oh, look at that.

The Dick has decided to make an appearance. "Orgasmic food?" he says. His eyes are laughing at me, and for two heartbeats, my uterus takes over for my heart, throbbing and channeling all my blood to my core.

"*Organic* food," I spit, even as I'm replaying my last tirade in my mind. Oh, H-E-double hockey fucks. I *did* say orgasmic food. Right before I told Crunchy's executive board to stick it up their asses. *Look what this man makes me do.*

"Get your head out of your dick," I snap. I'm already digging a hole, and I can't seem to stop shoveling deeper. "You have two choices, fuckwad. One, you issue an order telling everyone to mind their own fucking business while I go back and do my job, or two, I destroy you. You have ten minutes to make a decision and personally deliver it to me in the snack bar, where I'll be racking up a tab in your name."

I march to the door as if I could actually destroy him, which we both know I can't. He's a sexy, rich billionaire, and yes, I know that's redundant, but that's the part that makes him undestroyable.

That, and his mutant penis. The fact that he *has* a penis and I don't provides him with certain ridiculous protections, and the fact that it's mutant means he could make his next billion doing pornos.

"Rather bitchy, isn't she?" I hear one of the douchebags say.

One, *I'm a nice person.* I like puppies and kittens and I keep

44

a goldfish and an aloe plant. I call my mom and dad every Sunday, and the *only* time I flip anyone off in the city is when I'm driving.

Two, and more importantly— "How the fuck does a company as awesome to work for as Crunchy get such short-sighted, stuffy assholes on their executive board?" I throw over my shoulder.

The secretary applauds when I walk out. "I'd do him too, honey, and I wouldn't regret it."

"Great. You can have him. You can have *all* of them."

I will not cry. I will not cry. I will not cry.

I'll get on the elevator and ride it down to the snack bar where I'll drown my mortification in organic, pasture-raised, hormone-free yogurt sticks and fair trade, gluten-free, vegan chocolate chip cookies, but *I will not cry.*

I'll also deposit half my severance package in my cussing jar. Again, *see what the Dick makes me do?* I'm from Minnesota. *Fuck* is used sparingly, like pepper. Which is the *only* heat allowed *ever*, and never in pineapple tater tot casserole.

I set a timer on my phone for ten minutes—the last ten minutes I'll ever spend in Crunchy, undoubtedly—and clear out the snack bar. Every organic juice, every fair trade cocoa treat, every pesticide-free cobbler, I pile it all on my tray, grab three more trays to manage the load, and somehow I get it all to the cashier. "Bill it to Chase Jett," I tell her.

"Yeah, yours, mine, and hers," she says in a thick Brooklyn accent. Her fingers fly over the computer screen. "One twenty-five sixty. Cash or credit?"

"The Dick's paying for it." I dangle my employee badge, letting her get a good look at my name.

Her eyes go wide. Just as I suspected, the entire building knows.

"You the elevator chick?" she asks.

"Yep."

"They firing you?"

"Trying to."

She nods. "Go back and get some cheese biscuits too. Hormone-free. Taste like hockey pucks, but they freeze good for when you get hungry. I ain't seen nothing. Here's a bag for your goodies. Take six. Gonna need 'em. God bless ya, honey. Hope the screw was worth it."

I dump everything—plates and all—in reusable, organic-cotton Crunchy totes and drag my haul across the snack bar to an open table by the windows overlooking the tree-lined street. I'll miss this view. Not that I sat here and watched the street often, but I have this sinking feeling it's time to move home. My mom's been running an Etsy business selling mason jars with homey motivational sayings etched in them in preparation for retirement. I could move into the basement and help double her production. It's been ten years, and that restraining order for the Bratwurst Wagon will only really be a problem during Baloney Festival.

"Berger."

Would you look at that?

Mr. Fancy-Pants Twisted-Dick Billionaire himself has come to the snack bar.

I hug two bags to my chest. I'd hug them all if I were half the size of my brothers, but I got the short genes in the family and two's all I can hold without toppling myself over. Still, the Dick is *not* getting my cheese biscuits. Or anything else from me. Except a nod of acknowledgment. "Dickhead."

There are only four other people in the snack bar. All four of them gasp in unison. Chase's left eye twitches, and for a split second, I swear the right corner of his mouth twitched too.

Upward. Like a… Like a *smile*. As though he has a sense of humor.

Yep, I'm getting canned.

"Quit fucking around and get back to work. All that bok choy won't sell itself."

Glitter is all over his hands. It's decorating the bits of his soul stuck in his chin dimple. His suit coat sparkles like a leisure suit, and I have to pretend I remember yoga breathing to keep from snorting out a laugh. Swear to God, if his ass is covered in glitter, I'm buying Eloise a new drum set and Parker a new guitar.

Wait.

He just told me to get back to work.

Like I still have a job.

"Don't make me regret this," he growls. "I can make your life hell."

"You already do." I give him my worst fake smile and stand, still clutching the bags. The whole marketing department's having snacks on me today.

Well, on Chase.

But I had to sleep with him to get said snacks, so I'm still a giver.

His left eye is twitching again. Without another word, he turns and stalks out of the snack bar.

Glitter sparkles in a giant rainbow all over his ass.

What do you know?

Today *is* a good day to be me.

7

Chase

I HATE it when Bro's right. But she's so fucking right my nuts hurt. And not just because a glitter bomb exploded all over them when I sat down this morning.

She'll pay for that. She'll pay *dearly* for that. I don't even care if she didn't do it, she'll pay.

I'm picturing her spread out naked on the counter of the snack bar, in a fantasy that involves her tits again, and I realize I'm so totally fucked I can't see my way to getting unfucked.

I need to get my dick back in my pants and start using my head again, because I have housecleaning to do.

Mavis, the executive administrative assistant, is easily bought with a contraband chocolate chip cookie from Starbucks and a bullshit story about my sister getting fired from a job after filing a sexual harassment claim.

The only thing not true is the part about me having a sister. She was actually a girl I dated about eight years ago.

I might hate Bro like New Yorkers hate the Red Sox, and I might hate myself for wanting to fuck her brains out again—and again, and possibly again and again—but I won't tolerate the way my executive board was ready to fire her for what she drove me to in the elevator last night.

Takes two to have sex. Letting the woman take the fall isn't how I do business. Plus, my mother would be horrified.

Over everything.

Thank *god* she's halfway around the world.

By four, I have a stack of paperwork outlining at least a dozen cases of harassment or inappropriate relationships that have been swept under the rug with severance packages. I want to hit something.

Instead, I take a break to get out of the building and cool off, and something else hits me.

Namely, a fist. Right to my left cheek.

The ham-boned sucker punch isn't the first one I've gotten from this guy, who used to be like a brother to me, but the last time he hit me was a decade ago. Since then, he's been drafted by the NHL and beefed up even more than the stocky bull he used to be. In a battle of wits, he probably couldn't spell his name, but I like my skull in one piece, so I do the most manly thing I can. I lift a hand to order back the security guards flocking out of the building to defend my honor. "I got this, boys."

"Mr. Jett—"

"Back up or you're all fired."

They all stop. Nice to know where their loyalty lies. I think.

"Feel better?" I ask Ares.

"No way, motherfucker."

The term he's really looking for is *sister fucker*, but there's no sense in waving red panties in front of the bull. Dude takes his name seriously, and his twin brother isn't any better. Worse, actually, because he got the brains on top of the stature.

Later I'll contemplate the amazing feat that was Ares using a *four*-syllable word, but for now, I'm going to try not to get hit again.

"Sir, we're going to have to ask you to leave," the biggest of the Crunchy security dudes says. He has to crane his neck to make eye contact with the beast.

"Or I can crush you like a bug." Ares pushes a fist into his other palm and glowers. If he'd been born anywhere but Minnesota, he probably would've been a pro wrestler. In Minnesota, it's hockey first, nice second.

Since Ares can't count to two, all I get from him is the hockey glare.

I flip a look at the guard to my right. "Go tell Ambrosia Berger she has a visitor."

Suddenly my feet are dangling off the ground. "You don't say her name," Ares snarls. His breath smells like Cheetos and stale coffee, and his nose has more personality than it did last time. I added one of those lumps, but I knew him better then.

I'd also had an overwhelming and uncontrollable case of rage fueling my fists that day.

Don't get me wrong, I'm pissed about the shit I need to clean up at Crunchy. I'm also pissed that I let Bro drive me to fucking her in the elevator. But getting off last night seems to have put me in a mellow place.

Especially since I've come to my senses and realized there's no fucking way Ambrosia Berger would've let me stick my dick in her if she wasn't already on birth control.

She'd probably claim she was on STD-preventatives too, because she can't resist getting any random dig in, but I'm not planning on giving her the satisfaction of letting her throw that one in my face.

"How about putting me down?" I say to Ares. "Your sister can take care of herself. She glitter-bombed my office, and god only knows what she buried in my desk drawers to make that stench."

Ares loosens his grip, and my feet slip closer to the ground. "She got you with that sparkle shit?"

Aw, he said a two-syllable word. His mother will be proud. "All over my ass."

"Got my whole team too. In March."

He drops me. I land on my feet and take a subtle but healthy step out of arm's reach. "Heard you made the play-offs." I would've cheered against him and the Blackhawks, but they were battling his twin, Zeus, and the Predators, so it was pointless. I watched baseball spring training instead. "Nice."

"Sir?" The guard is back, and he looks like he's just swallowed a live frog. "Ms. Berger has, erm, declined to see her visitor. And you may consider updating the employee guidelines on profanity."

I can't exactly threaten to move her whole department into the elevator of shame with her brother standing here, frothing at the mouth. I like breathing. I'd like to continue breathing for the next sixty or seventy years. I box, I run, and I can bench my own weight, but Ares can bench an entire city block.

This calls for a far more subtle attack.

One that no one can fault me for, but that Bro will hate just as much as she probably hates working for me.

Psychological warfare is the shit.

"Too bad." I shrug. "I thought she'd enjoy having dinner at Selma's with her brother. On me."

"They eat raw shit there?" Ares asks.

"If you want."

"Like my steak raw," he grunts.

51

Not surprised. *Medium-rare* has too many syllables. And *well-done* sounds more British than ape.

I hate that I miss this dumbass, but I do. Zeus was the brains, Ares was the muscle. I was the spice.

My phone dings. It's a photo text of Bro's middle finger.

"Look at that," I say. "Your sister's decided to join you. I'll get a car brought around." I slap him on the back—not expecting that, is he?—and retreat before he can process what's going on. I glance at the frog-eating guard. "Might want to put stronger steel on the lower windows," I murmur.

Or I might want to sell this godforsaken grocery store.

But Bro would like that too much.

And I'm not getting out of organics. This isn't business.

It's personal.

8

Ambrosia

I PULL a seat up at the edge of the red velvet-lined booth at Selma's and picture my brothers having their nose hairs plucked out one by one. Ares is playing with the candle flame and taking up the entire right half of the booth, Zeus occupies the whole left half. I get a slice of the end.

"We already ordered two of everything," Zeus tells me. His leg is bouncing, which explains the vibrations I felt on the sidewalk outside.

"But what am I going to eat?" I ask.

That earns me two matching grins. "A knuckle sandwich," Zeus says.

A server approaches. He eyeballs my seat. These fancy places with Turkish rugs and real art and privacy curtains don't like it when you sit at the end of their booths. But then he takes stock of my brothers and bows his head in concession. "A drink, madam?"

"I'm not staying," I assure him. "Third wheel and all. But

did these two lovebirds order a bottle of your best champagne yet?"

He dips his head once more. "Not yet, madam. I'll see to it."

My brothers don't blink at the implication. Ares because he probably didn't understand it, Zeus because—never mind. I hate thinking about my brothers and their security in their masculinity, because *ew*.

"Ah, she's mad," Zeus says to Ares. "You should've waited for me. I had a plan to get rid of him without anyone knowing."

"The two of you together are as wide as a street. You can't sneeze in Brooklyn without the tremors reaching all the way out to Long Island, and you think you were going to somehow sneak stealthy revenge on a billionaire?"

"He impugned your honor," Zeus says.

"We can be small," Ares adds.

My brothers, ladies and gentlemen. I haven't seen them since they battled it out in the play-offs, and I miss the goobers. "How long are you in town? I have band practice tonight, but we could hit a Yankees game tomorrow."

And then I can pretend, for three glorious hours, that I didn't spend my day having my every move watched and whispered over by the people I'd claimed as family just yesterday. Everyone from the custodian to the store managers who were in the building for a social media crash course knew who I was and what I did in the elevator last night.

You know your life priorities are a little out of whack when what you're most grateful for is the fact that video hasn't leaked onto the internet. Without actual proof, I could twist this anyway I wanted to, and the only people who could correct me would be the security guards—whom I'm pretty sure only had a visual without the sound, please, god—or the Dick.

"Game sounds fun. Just us?" Zeus asked. "Or is the elevator fucker joining us?"

There go my panties getting damp at *that* part of the memory. *Thanks, Zeus.* And thanks to whoever's leaking the gossip outside the company. I don't want to know how they know. "Just us. Does Mom know you say *fucker*?"

"Who do you think taught me?" His eyes glint, and we all crack up. Mom saying *fucker* is about as likely as all of us sitting down over pineapple tater tot casserole for a round of Cards Against Humanity.

"She put sparkles on his ass," Ares tells Zeus.

Zeus has a wicked vengeance smile. "You got him with that glitter bomb shit?"

"This is a five-star restaurant, not a locker room," I say. Somebody has to pretend to be outraged other than the elderly couple behind us. "And no. *I* didn't plant glitter bombs in his office. But it might've been my idea. And I might've played lookout."

Both my brothers fist bump me.

I'm considering having a hundred cases of hot dog buns delivered to the Dick's office with a suggestion of where he can stick his sausage next time he feels an urge, but everyone had been watching me too closely at work for me to covertly manipulate the inventory and shipping systems.

He was eerily un-dick-like today. It's making me nervous. I think he's trying to screw with me.

"You need us, we're here," Ares says.

"Don't suppose you two can afford to buy an organic grocery store chain."

Ares digs a few thousand dollars out of his wallet and shoves it at me.

Zeus grins again. "Dude. It's way more than that."

A different server delivers the champagne, along with a tray of appetizers.

Both of my brothers remove their elbows from the table and stare as fine china plate after fine china plate elegantly decorated with small-portioned food art is placed on the black tablecloth.

Ares starts to open his mouth. I love my brother—and not only because he just offered me a stack of Benjamins for a down payment on a grocery store—but I know he's about to insult the food. I kick him under the table, and he closes his jaw. He might not be bright, but Mom drilled manners into all of us.

"Dated a girl once who ate shit like this," Zeus says after the server pours their champagne and departs.

"One?" Ares asks.

"One was enough."

Probably good that my brothers can't afford to buy Crunchy. They wouldn't get the customer base. Or the product.

Especially the vegetables.

Mom could only do so much with these two.

I take a plate with three edamame in the center of a small arrangement of watercress on a single slice of parboiled sweet potato and swallow it in one bite.

My brothers recoil in horror.

"Thanks for dinner," I say. "I'll get tickets to the game. You guys try to not harass anyone else I work with, mmm-kay?"

Ares levels a look that justifies his name. "He broke you."

See? How can I not love these guys? "It was ten years ago, and I made prison my bitch."

Okay, fine, by *prison*, I mean three nights in a county jail cell, and by *made it my bitch*, I mean I was reduced to a blubbering, scaredy-cat mess for those three nights, but I wouldn't be the woman I am today without the experience.

"My employment options are limited at the moment, so we're all going to play nice until he goes away, okay?"

"I'll get you a job," Zeus says.

"*I'll* get you a job," Ares says.

Zeus is in Nashville and Ares plays in Chicago. My police record and recent sexual exploits wouldn't make a hockey team blink, but as much as I love my brothers, I prefer food to their kind of mother puckers.

The food doesn't talk back or try to screw me.

Usually.

"I like New York and I like my job," I tell them. "This will blow over. I'm staying."

My brothers drop it. They convince me to stay through dinner, then we get takeout hamburgers for the two of them for dessert. Because they're goobers, they order a Zeus Berger and an Ares Berger, which confuses the heck out of the poor Five Guys cashier, but the guy manning the grill turns around and almost faints.

When he gets control of himself, he asks for selfies and autographs on his forehead, then triples their beef for free.

Zeus and Ares are the two biggest guys to ever play in the NHL. They're called the Twin Tanks, the Brute and the Force separately, and fans go stark raving nuts when they play each other. They once made ESPN for a private bet over who could bench the bigger cow. Literal *cows*. I'm pretty sure Ares could pull a tractor on a rope with just his teeth, and Zeus would undoubtedly try a 747 if Ares tried a tractor.

Tonight, after the Berger show at Five Guys, the two of them come with me to band practice and belt the hell out of N*SYNC's greatest hits. Parker goes a little star struck. Eloise bangs the drums while eyeing Ares like she'd like to bang him. Willow stops groaning over a wedding magazine to squeal, clapping her hands and asking if they can dance too.

The one thing we *don't* talk about?

Chase Jett.

It's two solid hours of heaven.

My brothers leave me at my apartment building. I assume they're heading off to a club that mere mortals like me don't know exists, and frankly, I'm exhausted to the point that I wouldn't care if the bass was thumping right in the center of my apartment.

I'm going to sleep like a baby tonight. Mating Hogzilla above me and all.

Except when I turn into my hallway, the Dick is leaning on the wall outside my door.

Waiting.

And probably not for Mrs. Byrony in 3C, or Buck and Jason next door.

Chase is in low-slung jeans and a fitted white button-down that tucks in at his slim hips and perfectly brings out the bronze in his skin. His deep-set blue eyes track my path, and the intensity radiating off him reminds me of a leopard on the prowl. He still has glitter in his eyebrows. My nipples tighten, my belly curls, and I catch myself about to lick my lips.

"Oh, honey," I say. "I should've warned you about my magic vagina. It makes men fall madly and irresistibly in love with me. The only way to break the spell is to dunk yourself in the Hudson four times at midnight under a full moon."

I'd like to dunk myself in the Hudson for wondering if he's at all turned on by the sight of me. Is that bulge natural, or do billionaires shop at special bulge-enhancing jeans shops?

It's natural, and you know it, Ambrosia May Berger. The man has a personal endowment for the arts in his pants.

"Are you on birth control?" he asks.

Mrs. Byrony pokes her head out. She's approximately a

century and a half old, her apartment smells like cinnamon and mouthwash, and her dog is the cutest thing on two legs. "If you two are talking about sex, take it inside. I just got dumped by a retired trash collector and I'm in no mood for love."

The door slams. Even from outside, I can tell Hogzilla and Wonder Boy are at it upstairs again. The squeaking is softer out here, but once you hear it, you can *never* unhear it. I push my key into the lock and open the door.

"Yes," I say. I don't add *Get lost, dickhead*, but only because I'm trying to be the better person. And partly because I'm wondering if he's asking because he wants round two.

I'm highly ashamed. Mortified. My vagina has lost its mind.

I step in my apartment and force the door closed, because I'm trying to think with my brain tonight.

I almost make it.

His foot is pretty solid. Sort of like his long, twisted, hard—

Argh.

"What do you want?" I say. Nicely. Or at least nicely enough to appease my mother during forced apologies after fighting with my brothers. I've mastered riding that line.

A fact that Chase apparently doesn't appreciate, because he looks like he'd rather dip his dick in cow dung and go wading through mosquito territory than be here with me. "How much do you know about management?"

Now I see why he's the billionaire and I'm stuck in low-level management. While I'm contemplating his dick, he's doing the hard businessman stuff.

Heh. *Hard.*

Not tonight, buddy.

I fling the door open and let him catch it himself. "Piss me off and I'll throw you out the window."

"Debating throwing myself out the window," he mutters.

"At least we're on the same page."

My apartment is your typical single-girl New York apartment. One room with kitchenette, living area, and bed— hidden behind a screen, because you can take the girl out of Minnesota, but you can't take Minnesota out of the girl— with a postage stamp bathroom fed by pipes that serve the dual purpose of water delivery and ghost housing. The way those things groan sometimes would honestly make Ares cry. He's terrified of ghosts.

Not that I'm allowed to say that out loud. Zeus would kick my ass.

Anyway, back to the apartment. I have exactly zero chairs and one couch, so I flop down and stretch out on it.

What? I'm tired, and it's his fault.

He gives me the eyeball of *Grow up, Bro* and takes a seat on my secondhand coffee table. It wobbles, but it doesn't give.

"What about management?" I ask. The sooner we're done, the sooner I'm going to bed.

Alone.

Squeaky-squeaky-squeaky-squeeeeeeeak.

Seriously, I'm writing her a note. First thing tomorrow. *Try the elevator.*

Sheesh, it's hot in here.

Chase clears his throat. "It's all male."

I blink, and it takes me a minute to realize he's talking about management and not his penis.

Which I'm well aware is *all-male.*

"Welcome to the twenty-first century," I say. About management. "No, wait… Yeah. Yeah, we're still here."

"Why?"

"Do I really need to explain this to you?"

"You have the most productive department in the building."

Did he just compliment me? I squint at him. "Are you really Chase Jett, or do you have a secret evil twin?"

"Cut the shit, Bro. You wouldn't have stayed at Crunchy if it were a terrible place to work. Your department is top-notch, but upper management is all cocksucking dickheads."

"I have a criminal record. I work where I can work."

He rolls his eyes so hard I'm surprised they don't get stuck in the back of his head. "Quit hiding behind that old bullshit."

"You told me to drive."

"I told you to get out of there."

"Ketchup, catsup."

Hogzilla lets loose with her mating call, and apparently she has a new Wonder Boy tonight, because an elephant trumpet answers her.

Chase blinks at the ceiling. "The mating hogs," he mutters to himself.

"Welcome to the broke New York life."

"You live under a fucking zoo."

He says it not like I live under a stupid zoo or a crazy zoo, but like I live under a zoo specially designed for fucking. He might be right. I should ask the building super how closely they check references. And species.

"You want to know about management, call Heidi Rumple. She's responsible for the cool marketing office, and she was on the fast track up the ladder when she quit to take a nanny job in Hoboken. Now go away. I can't sell bok choy if I can't sleep."

Squeaky...squeaky...squeaky...

A wild grunt that's more bearish than hoggish drifts through the ceiling. She's apparently having an animal orgy tonight. Maybe Willow's couch is open.

I could crash at my brothers' hotel, but I grew up with them, and I know how badly they can smell.

"We don't have to be like this," Chase says quietly.

"You didn't have to rig paintballs to rain down on me when I left the house for my first day of high school either, but you did."

"That was *fifteen fucking years ago*. And if you hadn't told my mother I jerked off in the cafeteria, I probably wouldn't have. You were *thirteen*. You shouldn't have even known the word *jerk off*."

"Then you shouldn't have taught it to me." And now I'm picturing him stroking his thick, bent penis, and I'm getting seriously wound up down south. I grit my teeth in frustration. This man is not good for me. Not as my brothers' best friend, not as my boss, and not as...whatever this is between us. "Seriously, why are you here? What do you want from me?"

His jaw is flexing and ticking, and I can't decide if he's also turned on, or if he's just pissed off.

Such a fine line between us, it seems.

"Information," he grits out.

"So you can destroy one more thing in my life?"

"Yes, Bro, I bought a whole fucking grocery store just so I could lay ruin to it and leave you without a job. You've found me out."

When he puts it like that, I sound like a spoiled brat.

But I wasn't the one who thought popping my Barbies' heads off and hanging them upside down in the fridge with ketchup dripping off them was *a good way to make friends*. Forgive me if I have a few trust issues.

"Everyone at Crunchy is there because we believe in the cause," I tell him. "What we don't know is if *you* do. You have a problem with management, it's just that. *Your* problem. You bought us. You want to fix what's broken, great. But don't you dare touch my team, because we're *good*, and you wouldn't have had a company to buy without us."

He stands, his hands fisted, elbows drawn in like he's trying not to punch something.

Probably because he knows I'm right.

And I know how much he hates that.

Which might possibly mean he's just as turned on as I'm trying to pretend not to be.

"Heidi Rumple. Thank you. Enjoy your mood music."

The door slams behind him.

I get ready for bed, but I'm hyped up on hormones and something else I don't want to identify—something that might be a niggling worry that Chase Jett just tried to come into my apartment and act *human*—and I can't sleep.

So I do the only thing guaranteed to put me out like a light. I climb under my covers, wriggle out of my panties, and slip my hand between my legs, rubbing myself and giving in to the ache that's been growing all night. Images of Chase in the elevator dance behind my eyes, and I picture him back in my living room, telling me my pussy is as rotten as moldy canned baloney, and I'd reply that his dick could be a case study for the Centers for Disease Control. He'd attack my mouth with his tongue, cup my pussy in his hands, shove his fingers—no, his whole hand—deep inside me, and now I'm picturing us on his desk in his office, my legs splayed while he licks my pussy and the whole office watches, and *oh yes*, I'd buck and writhe and scream and I'm wet and horny and my fingers aren't as big as his, I can't get as deep as he was last night, so I flick at my clit and grit my teeth and try to give Chase a different face while that slow, deep spiral builds in my core.

My fingers go faster, and I picture Chase and his crooked dick ramming into me, driving me wild, pounding hard and deep and full with his magnificent wonder cock, then Chase getting me off with his fingers again, him sucking on my pussy with that wicked tongue, nipping at my clit with his teeth—

I arch back in my bed as the orgasm rolls through me, but it's not enough.

It's not enough, and I'm pissed that it's not enough, because Chase Jett is somehow *ruining masturbation*. I reach into my nightstand for Bob and treat myself to a double header.

But it's still well past midnight before I finally fall asleep, and my subconscious is just as much of a traitor as my vagina.

9

Chase

I OPEN my front door Thursday morning expecting to see the car I ordered to take me to Crunchy, and instead find myself facing the blond-haired, blue-eyed Berger brothers. In a lot of ways, the family resemblance between them and Bro is strong. Norwegian coloring, the same mouth—though Bro's might be bigger—and they all piss me off by just breathing.

My stairs flare out to the ground until they're wide as the brownstone, but these two yahoos are completely blocking the sidewalk. I ate at their house as often as I ate at my own growing up, but whatever Mrs. Berger fed me couldn't have come from the same stock as what she fed her own boys.

Ares cracks his knuckles.

"You got a thing for Ambrosia?" Zeus asks.

If by *thing*, he means a confounding, raging hatred combined with a reluctantly growing amount of respect and an uncontrollable hard-on every time she opens her fucking mouth, possibly.

But I also still have a thing for breathing.

"If I say yes, are you going to pound me into the side-walk?" I will not be a pansy-ass billionaire who needs a personal bodyguard. I won't.

Zeus studies me. "No."

"If I say *no*, are you going to pound me into the sidewalk?"

"What's wrong with her?" Ares growls.

Zeus puts a hand to his chest and keeps him from charging up the stairs. "We were talking. Got to remembering all the pranks we pulled on her. How half of them were your idea."

"Sunny said you like her," Ares says.

I don't know who Sunny is, but based on the way they both smell faintly of whiskey and Ares's hair is standing on end, I'm going to guess they had a good time with her last night. And look at that, another two-syllable word.

"And considering how many times you've slept with her…" Zeus lifts a brow, asking me silently to give him a number.

Except there's a problem.

There's no *sleeping* where Bro and I are concerned.

Nope, that's all fucking. We've never even been close to a bed. No pillows. No sheets or blankets either.

Which I can't say to her brothers if I want to stay intimately acquainted with my pulse.

"What do you want me to say?" I ask.

"We miss you," Ares grunts.

I open my jaw, but no words come out.

"Used to have fun," Zeus says. "World's a lot more fun now. But it's missing something."

"Bro—*Ambrosia* doesn't like me," I say carefully.

These guys don't have guns for arms, they have Navy-issue, long-range cannons, and they simultaneously fold them over their barrel chests. Because I've just told these men their sister is fucking me despite her aversion to me, which more or less translates to me calling her a whore in bro-speak.

"Like that," I add quickly. "She doesn't like me like that." Bro's a lot of things, but she's not...*that*.

Their eyebrows simultaneously lower, and I realize I am not making this better.

"Yet?" I add.

For all I know, these two had a threesome with some random chick named Sunny last night. They're the *it* boys of the National Hockey League. If they're not getting laid regularly by puck bunnies, I'll suck my own dick.

But I can't have a night or two of mind-blowing sex?

Zeus breaks first. He drops his arms, but he's still giving me the big brother *I will tear your limbs off, starting with your dick, and make you eat them before I extract your teeth with a pair of rusty pliers* glare. "Got four tickets to see the Yankees tonight. Gates open at six. Be there."

Four tickets could mean one of two things. Either the two of them are squishing into three seats and leaving me the fourth, or Bro's coming too.

She might have a point about there being other organic grocery stores I could invest in. Unfortunately, *this* one is best suited for my long-range plans. I made my money in tech with the sole purpose of getting *here*. Coding is easy. It's logical. And—*thanks, Dad*—I have an intimate working knowledge of the psychological power of gaming addictions, which made *Frenemy Crush* a game I could've coded in my sleep.

My experience in the food industry, on the other hand, is limited to watching my mother almost kill herself working at the baloney factory. But I know logic, and I know social media, and between the in-house greens and the fucking amazing social media campaigns Crunchy runs, there's not another grocery store on the planet that I could've bought to position myself to change the world.

I salute the Berger brothers. "Looking forward to the game."

Ares snickers. Zeus grins. "Got some glitter in your fingernails, dude."

"Suck my dick."

They both snort like we're best buds again and amble down the street.

The Bro part is messy, but Zeus and Ares were my brothers. I spent the better part of the last decade getting to this level of professional success, and now that I have the world at my feet, I've realized I have very few friends I can trust implicitly.

My childhood buddies are successful in their own right. They don't need my cash. They don't need my connections. They don't need anything from me.

But they're willing to give me a chance.

I start to smile as I make my way to the car. As the driver holds the door for me, my phone rings.

Mom.

She knows.

I don't have to pick up the phone to know she knows. Her cruise ship has internet. The Mediterranean, the South Pole, hell, she could be on the International Space Station and the gossip would still reach her.

And I thought dealing with the Berger brothers would be tough.

How am I going to explain this to my mother?

68

Ambrosia

BECAUSE MY BROTHERS are my brothers, they emailed me before I ever rolled out of bed to let me know they'd gotten a box at Yankee Stadium for the game tonight. I shoot them back a note telling them to un-invite their puck bunnies, because Eloise would kill for box seats to a game, and if I'm bringing Eloise, I'm bringing Willow and Parker too.

Willow really needs a break from wedding planning, and I owe Parker more than I can ever repay for her sticking by my side at work the last two days.

Especially this morning.

Because my workplace is a normal, healthy workplace—in other words, a gossip factory—and because Chase Jett *lives* to make my life miserable, everyone's whispering about his company-wide memo announcing a change to employee handbook policies, effectively declaring anyone can sleep with whoever they'd like, preferably off company time and grounds, provided that it doesn't interfere with the work getting done. Also, people caught gossiping will be subject to violations ranging from having points docked off annual performance reviews to suspensions without pay, with the possibility of termination if the behavior doesn't cease.

I reply to his email after having Parker remove all references to him being a dick.

If your goal is to destroy office morale and turn us against each other, congratulations, you've just done in forty-eight hours what the entire executive board couldn't do in ten years.

He responded with another company-wide memo thirty minutes later announcing that the entire executive board had been sacked, and he'd be looking internally first for replacements.

He didn't add *now quit gossiping and get back to work*, but he might as well have.

We would've ignored a direct order far more efficiently.

Madison is supposed to be scheduling our series of posts for the Choy Joy ad campaign, but she's whispering to April, and unfortunately for Madison, her whisper voice is about as subtle as my brothers' whisper voices.

"I just don't get why she gets to stay," she says. "I mean, she had sex in the *elevator.*"

Right. Not my best moment.

But the whole room has heard, and I have to say *something.* I climb out of the beanbag chair and face my coworkers and the people who report to me. "Look, we all have sex. Some of us might like to pretend we don't, but it's a natural biological function. It's necessary for the continuation of our whole entire fu—freaking species. There's only shame in sex if we choose to let there be shame in it. We work for an organic grocery store chain, for god's sake. We're *Crunchy.* You ask me, we should have dedicated sex rooms on every floor. Embrace your sexuality. Love yourself. And then get back to work."

A slow clap starts from the doorway. Chase and three young-ish suits I don't recognize are all standing there with their faces twitching. The three of them looking up, anyway. Two are women. The last guy is staring at his shoes, but I can tell his face is beet red.

As is Parker's.

I mentioned I owe her big time, didn't I?

"I believe what Ms. Berger was trying to say," Chase says, eyes dancing, lips fighting a gallant battle against a smile as his clapping subsides, "is that no one should be ashamed of their sexuality. I'd like to reiterate that there's a line between comfort in your own sexuality and the harassment of others, which will obviously not be tolerated, but if the need arises, which I trust it won't, I hope we can openly discuss any matters of a sexual nature openly and honestly.

I open my mouth, and he holds a hand up.

"Also, I believe she meant a *nap* room. Which we'll be exploring as an option given scientific data to support the benefits of napping during work hours."

Gasps of delight go up through the room.

The Dick just made himself a hero yet again. Him and his giant…chin dimple. Which is still glittering, just for the record.

I'd be mad, but honestly, a nap room would *rock*. Plus, who cares about my sex life when we've just had management approve napping on the job?

He points at Parker. "Ms. Elliott? A moment, please."

"I'm on team Sia," she blurts.

"Your loyalty is commendable."

I jerk my head, telling her to go with the Dick, and she stumbles after him. My brothers are still in town, after all.

If he messes with my best friend, there will be hell to pay. And when I'm done with him, I'll send Zeus and Ares over just for fun.

The door shuts behind them. Everyone's hyped up on the idea of nap rooms, and me and my sex room seem to be forgotten.

Thank god.

A sex room? I don't know how I survived the elevator sex incident, but I am no doubt three heartbeats away from being called in by HR again. For something. Or everything.

And I'm obviously not the only one who thinks so, because a message request pops up from *Jett, Chase, CEO and Owner* before he could even be to the elevators.

A SEX ROOM?

Forget the sex room. His profile is a cartoon sex god. He's totally inflated his muscles, his dark hair *never* looks that shiny or perfectly styled, his chin dimple is dashingly rugged and glitter-free, and his avatar is fake tanning.

Okay, I lied.

I can't forget the sex room. And now I'm picturing myself using it.

With Chase.

What? I type back. *Like the world wouldn't be a better place if some people didn't get off on a regular basis?*

YOU CANNOT PUT A SEX ROOM IN THE WORKPLACE.

I know why he's yelling. It's hardly an appropriate suggestion, but I'm in deep now, and I'm in it to win, damn it.

Sex IS natural, I fire back. *If we were as relaxed about sex as we are about eating, sleeping, and going to the bathroom, maybe there wouldn't be such a stigma to it. Maybe if we talk about sex like we all have it—and we ALL do, and you know I'm right, don't make me draw you a diagram or pull security footage—and don't be all sanctimonious in pretending we don't, then maybe there would be a few more women sitting in your executive office like equals.*

I wait, but he doesn't reply.

I tell myself it's because he knows I'm right, and he has no logical, compelling arguments against sex rooms in the workplace leading to women's equality in management.

I also grab my phone and text Zeus. *Do you think the Rangers could use someone new in their marketing or social media departments?*

Thirty minutes later, Zeus hasn't replied, but a new message pops up from Chase.

You have issues.

Yes. Yes, I do. *It's because I grew up with you,* I type back.

And then I treat myself to a long lunch in the snack bar, where the cashier tosses two extra cookies on my tray and charges the whole thing to Chase.

"I agree," she tells me, even though I didn't ask. "Sex rooms are the way to go."

I get a fist bump and one more cookie, and I wonder if I'll be seeing her in counseling with HR too.

11

Chase

FOR EIGHT STRAIGHT HOURS, I've had images of Bro's sex room seared into my brain.

And she's in every last image.

Her legs spread in invitation on a red velvet chaise. Bent over an ancient metal desk, offering me her ass. In one, there's a Bro vending machine, and I keep putting dollars in so I can eat her like an ice cream cone. That one's a little weird, I confess.

It's possible I have a problem. I can't decide if I need to do her again and get her out of my system, or attempt to offer an olive branch and let my mother introduce me to that nice fifty-year-old woman she met on her cruise who would make a much better daughter-in-law than Ambrosia May *what the hell are you thinking* Berger.

That's what Mom always calls her. And my mother's a fucking saint. She doesn't cuss.

Ever.

I'm trying to think about my mother and *not* Bro Berger when I arrive at Yankee Stadium.

Unfortunately, she's the first thing I see.

Bro, that is. My mother's still on her cruise.

Ambrosia's sandwiched between her brothers, a little speck between two boulders, but I see her first. She's doing what she always did when we were growing up—she's laughing.

She was always laughing with her brothers. Maybe not *always*—she didn't like it when they strung her craft beads on their used dental floss. Or when we used her flowery hair things as fishing bait. Or when Ares would fart on her dolls' heads.

But when her brothers weren't terrorizing her, or when she wasn't putting itch cream in their jock straps or honey on their field hockey sticks—all those mosquitoes in the summer, and Ares and Zeus always scratching down their pants and getting honey on their nuts... I *still* have nightmares for them.

Point is, she never smiled at me. She never laughed with me. She had this perfect little life, smart parents with good jobs, a big house, and two brothers who'd pummel you first and ask questions later if they thought you looked at her wrong. But she was always too good for me, and she thought her brothers were too.

She was probably right.

But look at me now, baby.

She catches my eye, and her smile drops off.

That's Bro Berger for you. Still too good for the riffraff from the wrong side of the tracks.

A billion fucking dollars in my bank account, and she's the only person in the world who sees me.

Zeus lifts a hand and waves to me. "Hurry up, dude. Beer's waiting."

"Why is he here?" Bro asks.

"I got bored." Zeus grins at her. "You gonna give us a show?"

"I'm giving you spiders for Christmas," she hisses. "Except I'm going to send them in October when you're not expecting them."

The woman knows how to terrorize her brothers, and don't let anyone tell you differently.

We're escorted in through the players' entrance. Fucker didn't get four seats, he got a private suite, which is good since Bro brought three friends. And my fat bank account is still new enough that I might buy grocery stores, business suits worth more than my hometown, and small pharmaceutical firms doing experimental research in combating the effects of pesticides and factory chemicals, but being treated like royalty still gives me a thrill.

Bro takes a seat in the two short rows of stadium seats at one end of the room, which would be comfortably-sized if we were all buddies, but are definitely too small for the seven of us. Her friends take the seats around her after grabbing snacks and drinks from the trays and buckets set out on the bar along the back wall.

I know Parker from Crunchy—she has two masters degrees, one in business administration and the other in marketing, fifteen years of experience, and she's been stuck in a worker bee job for years.

Not because she wasn't applying for promotions, but because she kept getting passed over.

I'm fixing that.

The other two women, I don't know at all, but the one who reminds me of Snow White with long hair is vaguely familiar. The shorter one with the spiky hair and librarian glasses strikes me as the terrifying sort, and not in the good way.

Zeus hands me a beer and straddles a chair. "She's avoiding you, man. What'd you do?"

Ares is behind me. He crushes a full beer can with his bare fist. Beer drizzles into my hair and down my neck. I jerk out of the seat. I could probably take him down with a well-aimed glass bottle, but at least when we were kids, there were only three places where his body was actually vulnerable, and two of them I wouldn't touch with a ten-foot pole.

"Hey, you're wasting good beer," Zeus says. "Knock it off and drink it like you have opposable thumbs."

Ares is twisting the can in his hands, grinning. "I did it."

Zeus does a double-take. "Oh, hey. You did." The brothers share a fist bump. "And that was one of the steel cans."

"That was so fucking cool," the spiky-haired one with Bro says.

"Don't encourage him." Bro points at Ares with the death finger that her mother used to use. "If you sleep with any of my friends, so help me, I will rub ghost chilis all over your mouth guard, smear Icy Hot in your cup, and I'll call ESPN and tell them you still wet the bed."

That, too, is classic Bro. And now my dick is sword fighting my zipper. I know what she can do when she channels that passion.

"What if he pours beer on Chase again?" Zeus asks with a smirk.

"Why would I care?"

"*Sia,*" Snow White chides in a whisper.

"*He's the numero uno dick-o,*" Bro whispers back.

"I know, but still…"

Her other friend, the scary one, points at me. "Hey, you've got some glitter right here." She pulls her eyelid over her eye.

Parker ducks her head over a bag of peanuts. Snow claps her hand over her mouth, but I still hear giggles.

Bro, on the other hand, is watching me like she knows what's up in my pants.

"You make her scrub the toilets at work or something?" Zeus says. "Man, she hates toilet duty."

Good to know. "We had a disagreement about employee motivation factors." Getting into details go could one of two ways. Either Zeus and Ares toss me out the front of the suite for saying *sex room* in relation to their sister, or the NHL gets a new idea in their suggestion box.

Possibly both.

"You do what she says if you want to keep her." There's three hundred fifty pounds of unpredictable Viking telling me to let his sister have a sex room at work. One day we'll look back on this and laugh. Or my dick is going to split the zipper in my jeans as it votes in favor of Bro's idea.

Zeus's eyes narrow. "I'm serious, dude. She asked us to find her a job with the Rangers."

"The fuck she did," I say before I realize which head I'm talking with.

"Free world, dickhead," Bro says, earning another poke from Snow. "*They'd* take my suggestions seriously."

"Fine." I'm sweating like a Canadian in Florida. I have *got* to get a grip on this throbbing in my nuts. Even if I'd prefer she get a grip on my nuts. Fucking Zeus and his *You like my sister, don't you?* "Send it through HR."

Parker, who I belatedly remember knows *exactly* what we're talking about, chokes on a peanut. We all hop up and fight over who's going to give her the Heimlich, and for once, my dick gets the memo that something honest-to-god serious is going on and gives me some breathing room.

Zeus grabs me by the collar and dangles me to get me out of the way. "I got this," he says.

Ares grunts and digs an elbow into his ribs, tripping over the seats.

"*Stop it,*" Bro shrieks. "You two yahoos will put her breast-bone through her spine before you get the peanut out."

"I like breasts," Ares says.

Parker's coughing and sputtering. Snow gives her a good hard whack, and peanut chunks fly across the box.

"Water," Parker rasps. She points at the Berger twins. "No touchy. *Nooo* touchy."

Bro shoves a bottle in her hand, Zeus signals Ares to sit, and I ease back into my seat, being careful with my tender balls.

I definitely have a problem.

Once everyone's certain Parker isn't going to choke again, the game's about to start. We stand for the National Anthem, and the scary one—Eloise, I've learned—whoops and hollers for every last one of the Yankees as they're introduced, even the batting manager. "He is *so* hot," she says.

The first batter goes up, and Zeus pokes me with an elbow that would probably earn him a trip to the penalty box if he were on the ice. "Hey, man, you remember that time we buried all of Ambrosia's troll dolls with just their hair sticking up and threatened to run over them with Dad's old push lawnmower?"

Bro's eyes take on a nuclear glow, and I have to shift in my seat to accommodate my once-again growing lightning rod. "Sure," I say to Zeus.

"Pink one was scary," Ares grunts.

"Not like that unicorn on her school binder." Zeus shudders. "The one with the rainbow horn? Something wrong with its eyes."

"There wouldn't have been if you hadn't put devil eye stickers over the real eyes," Bro says. "You possessed my unicorn."

"No, it was freaky before it got possessed. I wouldn't touch that thing." He slugs Ares. "That you?"

"No way. Scary horse bad."

Bro's looking a little possessed herself, and my balls are aching again. Pretty sure I can't solve this problem with a quick trip to the bathroom either. As long as she's within a quarter mile radius, and pissed off over *anything*, I'm going to be worse off than if I were force-fed a handful of little blue pills and tossed in a sultan's harem.

"Your handiwork?" she says to me, and now I'm thinking of her handiwork. Her hands. On my cock. Squeezing. Stroking. Guiding it to her mouth—

"You would've known if it was me," I say.

It was definitely me. And I would've hit the kitten posters in her room with them too if I'd known it bothered her.

For the first time in my life, I wonder if I was a shithead.

Always proudly claimed hellion. Never considered shithead. It's enlightening. Not sure how I feel about this.

Ares crushes another beer can.

While I move yet one more seat closer to the women, Eloise abandons Bro to claim the seat beside Ares. "Can you do two at once?" she asks.

"With my eyes shut," he says.

"Hold on." Zeus lifts his phone. "Let me get this on camera. Fellas ain't gonna believe this shit without proof."

I move one more seat down, but I'm grinning.

Because *damn*. I've missed these nimrods. "They don't change, do they?" I say to Bro.

"Nope. But they hit harder now."

Just like old times.

I chuckle to myself, steal a handful of her popcorn, and settle in to watch some baseball.

12

Ambrosia

CHASE JETT just smiled at me. It's not enough that he tortured me through childhood. It's not enough that he has enough money to buy a jet to fly to his personal Caribbean island and build his own private Disney World on it. It's not enough that I've been wondering how deep I could shove my tongue into his chin dimple.

When he smiles, fairies sing and the sun shoots glitter on its light beams and magical, happy, non-possessed unicorns fart rainbows across the sky.

I've never seen him smile—excluding all the times he did his evil overlord laugh whenever he'd get one up on me—and I don't like it.

And no, I don't want to discuss if it's his smile I don't like, or the fact that I've never seen it.

I also don't like that he's wormed his way into the seat beside me, with his long legs stretched out and crossed at the ankles, his wide shoulders edging into my personal bubble, with a swell in his crotch that's making me unfortunately horny. Just a little. Like a subtle swelling in my breasts that are making my barely tight nipples strain sort of-kind of loosely-painfully against my lace bra. Like a barely noticeable, pulsating, volcanic throb between my legs. Like a whisper of a hint that I might possibly desperately need to straddle him and rub my aching, swollen clit all over his long, thick shaft and—

Yeah. I'm just a little horny. Barely noticeable over—wait. When did Willow start talking to him?

"I get diversification," she's saying, "but a grocery store?"

"Everybody eats," Chase says.

"Not organic, free-range, fair trade, yada yada pricey pricey food."

He smiles that ridiculously handsome smile at her, and I can't decide if I want to slug him or mount him. His teeth are straight and perfect, like he must've gotten braces in the last ten years. The chin dimple makes his full lips seem manly and rugged, even with the glitter still stuck in there, and his eyes are crinkling like he's hiding a sense of humor in his blackened soul.

Which will only come out a muddy gray in my mind, because even I can't find the evil in this smile.

"I grew up on canned baloney." He winks at her. "Call it a billionaire's eccentricity if you want, but I have plans. Ten years from now, Crunchy's going to be the place even low-income families can go to get fewer pesticides and hormones in their food supply."

The crowd suddenly groans, and we all leap to our feet as a ball sails out of the park. Those of us from Minnesota, anyway, so basically me, my brothers, and Chase. Home run for the visitors.

"Yeah, *baby,*" Zeus yells. Ares is doing his war cry, a deafening howl that sounds like a flock of chickens being murdered. Huh. Maybe he could stop by my apartment about three AM and demonstrate for Hogzilla. And why hasn't this ever occurred to me before?

Oh, right.

Because I don't want to get kicked out of my building. Finding an affordable place in the city is akin to finding a new job when you have a criminal record and a current listing as a smokin' hot *do me now* mama on *Billionaire-Bangers.com*.

Still, it's tempting.

And it's taken my mind off the fact that Chase is pumping a fist and hollering as the Twins go up three to nothing in the first inning.

"What is *wrong* with you people?" Parker says.

"Minnesota proud," I reply with a shrug.

"From Philadelphia, my ass," Eloise grunts.

"Pittsburgh," Parker corrects.

"Pennsyl-whatever," Eloise fires back. "I can't believe we believed you."

She has a point, but it's been a decade since I've wanted to cheer for the Twins. Now that I've reclaimed my heritage, I couldn't stop myself if I tried.

Going to Twins games was a *huge* deal when I was little. Mom and Dad would take a day off work, we'd drive down to Minneapolis, have sandwiches in the car, and sit in the bleachers where we could each pick *one thing* from the snack bars. I'd go for cotton candy. Zeus and Ares would try to scam their way into more food, saying it was only *one* thing if they stacked their hamburgers between two large pretzels as bonus buns.

Chase went with us once. He got a bag of peanuts and spent the whole game tossing shells into my hair when my parents weren't looking.

Zeus and Ares never went to ball games with Chase's

family. Or to the lake. Or camping. Not like he'd tag along with us.

It never occurred to me that the only way he got to do all those things was with us. That his parents couldn't afford it. I'm sure his mom didn't make much, and I never gave a thought to what his dad did.

Or that he might've grown up on canned baloney, and buying Crunchy was his way of never having to eat it again.

He was right. Billionaires get to do the weirdest things.

Or possibly I'm spending too much time thinking about the guy who's sliding his arm behind my back at the baseball game.

I go stiff as steel on the outside and wobbly as my grandma's blue-ribbon gelatin mold on the inside.

Why is Chase Jett putting high school moves on me?

That volcanic throbbing in my nether regions is back. Lava's flowing, people. Chase Jett is touching me and my body is betraying me and—

Holy organic sausages, he's threading his fingers through my hair. Electric sparks light up my scalp, and I have to squeeze my lips together to keep from moaning. Squeezing my thighs together isn't doing much good either.

I wonder what he'd do if I follow him home. Or if I just show up naked on his doorstep. I could lob a few insults, question his choice in décor, call his dick some names, and he'd probably do me in the foyer.

What the hell is wrong with me?

My head is suddenly slapped forward. "*Ow!*"

"Knock it off, dickhead," Eloise says. She dangles a peanut shell in front of my eyes. "Sorry about the slap. He was putting this in your hair."

I yank his ear and twist. His head flops into my lap, but he's grinning. *Oh*, he's grinning. A delicious, dark, *spank me, baby* grin. "Your hair's boring. It needed some glittering up."

"You're dead," I grit out.

Ares snorts. "I see it too," he says to Zeus. The two of them share a smile and a fist bump.

I have no idea what they're talking about. Chase apparently does. He flips a double bird at them.

I'm suddenly reliving my childhood, except it's oddly non-traumatic.

"Can I have my ear back?" Chase says.

"Parker. Hand me a peanut. I need to shove it up his ear canal."

"Is it orgasmic?" Chase asks. "I only like orgasmic peanuts in my ears."

"I hate you," I say, and I'm horrified to realize I'm smiling back at him.

I drop his ear and shove him away.

Fine. Maybe he's not the devil.

But he's still not good for me.

13

Ambrosia

By the sixth inning, the Twins and Yankees are tied at four runs apiece. Eloise is acting like a puck bunny and hanging on Ares's every word. I shouldn't be surprised—she's always gone for the guys with a limited vocabulary.

Parker and Zeus are in a contest to see who can catch the most peanuts—Parker's winning, twenty-three to seven—and Chase has discovered Willow's stepdad is an honest-to-god king of a small Nordic country, and he's grilling her on the country's economy. Give a guy a billion bucks, and suddenly he thinks he can hobnob with royalty.

Entitled prick.

As for me, I'm trying to enjoy the game. Dusk is settling, it's seventy-two degrees, and it's anybody's ballgame.

What more could I want?

I mean, it's not like I want Chase to yank me by my hair like a Neanderthal, drag me into the bathroom and make him besmirch my already tattered honor.

That would be crazy.

It's not like I've been sitting here for five innings getting more and more turned on every time the man laughs. Or like I've been eyeballing that bulge in his pants, wondering how much longer he can go before *he* explodes or if being a billionaire somehow gives him magic junk that swells purely to torture the nearby women without causing him any discomfort. Or like I've been wondering if there's any way I could slip my hands into my pants to take some pressure off without anyone noticing.

It's his cologne, I've decided. His newest form of warfare. Odorless pheromones.

I need to steal his recipe. Bottle it and sell it with mobile sex rooms, and then *I'll* be a billionaire too.

Or possibly incarcerated again for breaking some obscure pheromone drug and sex peddling laws. *Thanks, Chase. Two trips to the pen, all courtesy of you.*

I growl at him.

He shifts his attention back to me and lifts a brow.

As if he doesn't know I'm on to him and his unscented, Ambrosia-targeting pheromones that are making me consider criminal activities.

I roll my eyes.

He grins, but this isn't the smile he's been giving Willow.

No, this is a smile of victory. Of power. Of corruption.

That's right. Corruption. Sexual corruption. All heavy-lidded and smirky and *has he always had those long eyelashes?* and holy sex on a stick *what the hell is wrong with me that I want to bang this man blind?*

I lift my chin and look away, and suddenly Zeus is punching me in the arm. "Kiss Cam," he hisses. "*Kiss Cam.*"

We're mid-inning and the crowd's chanting *Kiss her, Kiss her, Kiss her.* I lift my gaze to the video board, expecting to see a saggy grandma and gramps or some cute college couple, and instead, I'm staring straight at myself.

And Chase.

Zeus's giant fist is gargantuan on the screen, poking me hard enough to make my whole body shake. *"Kiss Cam*. You have to kiss. It's a rule."

Fine. It's a rule. I have to kiss Chase. Because the baseball gods demand it.

I'll do it. But I'm not going to like it.

I turn to him, and see my exact thoughts written in his eyes. *Bet you flinch first.*

He was *so* on.

I lunge at him before he sees it coming. My lips smush against the side of his mouth. My arm bangs the back of his chair. Someone shrieks, and I wonder if my beer is now decorating the suite.

That's the last rational thought I have before Chase grips my hair, guides my lips to his, and does that holy toe-curling, mind-bending, mouth-orgasm-inducing thing with his tongue. It's as twisted as his dick is, and *oh my god*, I want to suck on it until I can't feel my lips anymore, except then I couldn't feel the glorious way his twisted, wet velvet mouth-dick is making my entire body light up like a flashing neon video board strung with a billion Christmas lights.

Pleasure here, enter now and suck face until your ovaries explode.

There's an armrest between us, and that won't do, nope, absolutely won't do at all. I fling my leg over his leg—*god*, I ache, just one little touch, one little stroke, *please, I'll be a good girl and only call you a dick to your face when we're naked and not in an elevator and*—oh.

Oh, yes.

I don't care if that's his hand or the armrest or if it's a fucking bratwurst, something's rubbing my clit and he's still fucking my mouth with his tongue and he has an iron grip on the back of my neck and I can't breathe but I don't want to because *yes*, yes yes yes, more, *right there*, don't stop, oh my god, I'm rocking on his leg, or his arm, or something, and it's perfect and I'm suddenly remembering that thing he did with his hand in the elevator and I'm wet and hot and ready and I need to touch him.

I need to touch his cock *right fucking now*.

I uncurl my hands from fisting his shirt and tug the fabric out of his pants, seeking, searching—

And beer rains down on my head.

I jerk up.

Just in time, too, because Ares has dropped the twin beer cans he just crushed over our heads and he's grabbing Chase by the back of his shirt and lifting him like he's a feather. Or maybe a small bird. Or maybe a guy about to be murdered by an angry, three-hundred-fifty-pound brother whose day job is being a monster on and off the ice.

Someone screams.

I'm pretty sure it was Parker, but it might've been me, because it's totally worth screaming over the way Ares looks like he's contemplating tossing Chase out of the suite.

Right there.

At the edge of the suite.

Just drop him six stories onto the unsuspecting fans below.

"Out the *door*, dumbass," Zeus bellows.

My heart is simultaneously in my gut and in my throat, my legs are the consistency of melted jelly beans, and I can't catch my breath.

Ares twists Chase and stares him right in the eyeball, close enough that they both go cross-eyed. "That's my sister," he growls.

"And she's a big girl who can kick your ass," Chase growls

back as if Ares doesn't have at least eight inches and well over a hundred pounds on him and *why am I thinking about inches and pounding and getting turned on again?*

"Holy fuck," Eloise whispers.

I'm simultaneously mortified and lustified. And if you don't think *lustified* is a word, trust me, it is, and I am *so* that right now. Hornified too, which is like being horny and horrified all at once.

And I can't make up any more words, because I'm going to throw up because *Ares is going to throw Chase out of the box.*

"Ares, put him down," I order, but I sound like a sex-crazed nympho at a dildo party.

I don't know. I'm not thinking straight. Just go with it.

And for God's sake, *someone make my brother put Chase down.*

Either Ares reads my mind, or I shriek that last part out loud, because he finally puts Chase down. In the doorway. Which he flings open for the sole purpose of shoving Chase out of the suite, and then slams it shut again.

"You called him *Chase*," Ares says. "Not *Dick*."

Oh, shit. Oh, double hornified lustified shit.

He's right. I didn't call Chase a dick.

I like to think it's because I'm a nice person, but the truth may be far more sinister—and hornifying—than that.

Zeus is looking at me with his hockey game face. I've seen that face make grown men cry. I've seen that face make *lumberjacks* cry. It would probably make God cry, but for other reasons that aren't really relevant now because Zeus *does* exist and that *is* God's fault.

But that face won't make me cry, because I know Zeus is ticklish on his third rib and that he's terrified of daddy long legs, which I silently communicate back to him.

"You have a problem," he says.

I toss my hair. "I just wanted him to think he was doing a good job. It's my charitable act of the day."

I have a problem.

My phone dings somewhere in the suite. My three wide-eyed friends all lunge for the floor in front of the chair that probably needs to be disinfected or burned, and all three of them simultaneously gasp.

"Oh my god, Sia, you have a problem," Parker whispers.

"We've established that," I start, but my brain catches up quickly.

The Kiss Cam.

We just dry-humped *on the freaking Kiss Cam*. It's probably already on Facebook and YouTube. *My mother's going to see this.*

My fingers go numb.

Thankfully, so does my vagina. *Would've been nice five minutes ago, vagina.*

"What country did you say your mother married into?" I whisper to Willow. "And do they need a social media manager?"

Parker shoves the phone at me. "Hide this from your brothers. I'm taking you home. And *making sure you stay there.*"

I glance down, read the message, and every last inner muscle Chase hit the other night clenches in anticipation.

Mortification be damned.

Chase just texted that he has a sex room. And that I'm welcome to join him in it anytime.

Chase

BRO DOESN'T TEXT me back. She doesn't drop by my place, doesn't bang on the door to wake me up at some ungodly hour in the middle of the night—*bang*, that'd be funny except I didn't get any last night—and she hasn't booby-trapped my office with glitter bombs or rotting fish or lingerie that smells like her pussy.

It's like I don't exist to her.

She's so fucking good at fucking with my mind.

I spend the next morning interviewing candidates for the executive board. I'm going to have to go outside the company for some positions, but there's a lot of talent internally, and as I explain to each of my prospective board members my long-range goals for Crunchy, I'm also getting re-invigorated. When I'm done, there won't be any more canned baloney. No more chemicals hiding in our food and manufacturing processes to make people sick—those canning it *or* those eating it. Or those doing both. No more kids going hungry in schools either.

What good is being among the world's richest men if you can't solve a food supply problem?

And before you start throwing shit—I'm not putting people or industries out of work, either.

I'm going to buy them and fix them.

All of them.

Because I fucking can.

I'm in the middle of interviewing Tina, the world's perkiest woman, for a position in sales management when I hear a commotion break out in the lobby. My door flings open. "Gentlemen, you can't just go in there," my admin assistant says as thirteen-plus feet and seven hundred pounds of Viking hockey players get stuck battling each other to get through my door first.

"They're harmless," I tell Tina.

I hope I'm not lying.

"Oh my god, it's the Brute and the Force," she whispers reverently.

Zeus wins the battle of the doorway and strolls in first. He whips out a Sharpie, signs Tina's head, and then scrawls his name across my desk before doing a mic-drop with the marker. "We need to talk."

Ares adds his signature to Tina's left arm and eyeballs the front of my desk in a way that makes me think he's using X-ray vision to locate my crotch.

To sign it or turn it into ground meatballs is anybody's guess.

"Thanks for your time," I say to Tina. "I'll be in touch."

"If we had a sex room, I'd so be using it right now," she whispers reverently as she stumbles to her feet. "Can I get a picture before I go?"

I take her phone and snap a picture of Zeus and Ares

holding her mermaid-style, then a normal one with her dwarfed between the two men. If they have time for pictures, they're probably not here to chop my legs off.

When the door shuts, Ares sits in the leather chair Tina's just vacated. It creaks, there's a snap and a plume of glitter, and suddenly he's in a crumbled pile of old leather, springs, and wood that's seen better days.

Like yesterday, before a behemoth squashed it with his ass and released one last hidden glitter bomb.

"Dude," Zeus says. "We talked about you and chairs. What's the rule when you don't know where it's been?"

"Don't sit in it." Ares hangs his head.

I offer him a chocolate from the glass candy dish my admin insisted I needed. He swallows it, wrapper and all, then grabs the bowl and drinks the rest down.

I've mentioned I missed these guys, haven't I?

"You're my fucking hero," I tell Ares.

He grunts and eyes the candy dish like he's contemplating taking a bite of it too. We all ignore the glitter flickering through the air and coating us.

"You need help," Zeus says to me.

I pretend I don't know what he's talking about. "You quitting hockey to be my security guards?"

"No, fucker. But I know a few guys who retired last year and wouldn't mind that kind of work. I'll get you their names. They take orders well from smaller men. Sometimes. When the money's right."

"Much obliged."

"He means *thanks*," Zeus translates for Ares. He looks back at me. "And you need help with Ambrosia."

If by *help*, he meant electric shock therapy treatments to get over this growing obsession that started in my dick and spread to my brain, I'm inclined to agree.

"Come again?" I say, then wince.

Ares snickers, but it's his *you're two steps from fucking up and I'd be happy to use you like a nail that needs to be pounded into concrete with Thor's hammer* snicker. Dude talks in small sentences, but he does his silent communication in metaphor. It's one of the things we love about him.

"Flowers," Zeus says. "Wine. Candlelight. You need to woo her right."

There's something wrong about a freakishly large beast telling me I need to *woo* his sister. I rub a hand over my mouth to keep from telling him his sister is a pain in the ass and that his flowers, wine, and candlelight would all be seen as tools of psychological warfare and take me backwards in my quest to get back in her pants.

Or skirt.

Hell, I'd even take her in monk's robes, a tutu, or a shark costume. Or all three together. At this point, I'm not too picky. I just need to do *something* to return to her puss —ah, the land of sane, functioning, rags-to-riches busi-nessman.

Getting off is great, but *He was a man who had sex, and lots of it, and in the worst locations, with the woman of his nightmares* isn't the inscription I want on my tombstone.

Alright, fine, it could be an addendum. Having that carved in stone over my cold, dead body for all of eternity would be pretty fucking cool.

But I also want to be remembered for changing the world. *Outside* of the bedroom. And elevator. And private suite at Yankee Stadium. And on a pile of hundred dollar bills at the top of the Empire State Building, which I haven't done yet, but a man can dream.

I tug at my collar. Zeus is spot-on.

I have a problem.

"Are you imagining my sister naked?" he growls.

Now I am.

Okay, fine, yes. I was before too. "Why do you want to help me?"

"We help you, you help Ambrosia."

"Bro doesn't need help from anyone."

"That what you think?"

"We *are* talking about the woman who once walked two miles in the woods, in the dark, in the rain, to plant fake spiders around our campsite just to hear you scream like a girl the next morning, aren't we?"

Ares grins. "Last fall. Fun times."

I choke on a laugh. "She did it *again*?"

Ares holds up four fingers while Zeus punches him in the shoulder. Glitter sparkles on both their T-shirts.

"Go on and laugh," Zeus says. "But next time you see her, ask her about Vassar. Then tell me she doesn't need anything."

The Berger twins leave a glittery path of destruction on the way out of my office. The security guards are terrified, Zeus barely stops Ares from eating one of the potted plants —all for show, Ares hates vegetables—and I've just been tasked with fixing Bro's life when I didn't even know it was broken.

Three days ago, I wouldn't have cared.

Mavis strolls in and refills my candy jar as though handling Viking candy jar murders is a standard part of her job description. "Your mother's holding for you on line two," she says. "If I were you, I'd buy a florist and a candy shop. Maybe a winery too. Sounds like she needs them."

Might be time to resign from my personal life.

15

Ambrosia

FRIDAY NIGHT, Parker, Eloise, Willow, and I have a gig booked at O'Farrell's Irish Pub and I'm hoping they're paying in straight tequila.

"How are the wedding plans?" I ask Willow as we get prepped in a storage closet behind the stage.

She huffs out a sigh. "Martin can't decide which invitations he likes best, there's a big to-do over whether or not the king's stepdaughter should be allowed to get married in the abbey, not that anyone's asked _me_ if I want to get married in the abbey or if I'd prefer a nice quiet ceremony on a boat in the fjords, or, you know, to have it _here in New York_, and Martin's great-aunt Greta sent me a box of vintage seventies lingerie _that she expects me to model and send her pictures of_. Oh, and I caught my landlord pawing through the box in the lobby. He says it was open and he was checking it for bombs."

We all blink at her.

"You want me to take care of him?" Eloise offers.

"As soon as we're married, I'll move in with Martin, and all of this will be a distant memory."

They're waiting for marriage to move in together. It's kinda sweet, except for the part where it took Martin seven years to propose. Among other things.

"Enough of the wedding." She straightens a brass Buddha on the shelves. "Did work get better this week?"

As long as Chase Jett owns Crunchy, I'm fairly certain work there will never be *better* for me.

"I cold-called the Rangers today," I announce. "They said, and I quote, *Sia Berger? Riiiiiiight. Good luck with your medication, honey.*"

"Ridiculous," Eloise says. "The Kiss Cam shut off before the show went X-rated. This is discrimination."

"No, this is my brothers. Fifty bucks says Zeus told them a crazy woman pretending to be his sister would call and ask about a job."

"Your brothers are so fucking cool."

Parker scowls at me. She's on a stool, and she gives one of her guitar's tuning knobs a vicious crank. While I spent today getting shit for the Kiss Cam video—which, yes, went viral within five seconds and I've had to talk my mother off a ledge at least six times a day the last two days—Parker was getting promoted to head of marketing. A position she totally deserves and will completely rock at, but also a position I might've been considered for if, you know, *Vassar*. And no Grand Theft Bratwurst Wagon on my record.

"You are *not* quitting Crunchy," she says. "First of all, you're brilliant and we need you. Second, you're being an excellent role model with all of the discretion you've shown in refusing to talk about Chase at work. If you exclude whatever's going on with you and the snack bar lady, anyway. And third, if you leave, I'm going to drill holes in your apartment ceiling so you can hear Hogzilla's mating call even louder."

"You *wouldn't*."

"Oh, I would." Parker could've easily been my older sister. She's strong, she's devious, and while she'll rip me to shreds when it's just the two of us, she'll defend me to the end against outside evil, and I'd do the same for her.

"I'd help her," Willow says. "Chase has some really great ideas for Crunchy. My mom said he talked to my stepdad this morning. The king has some holdings in US agriculture, and he's apparently considering some kind of partnership. Sia, I know it's been a rough week, but you've always loved Crunchy. Don't do anything rash, okay? I'd hate to see you miss out on an amazing opportunity at a company you adore just because of a man."

I'm doing my best to ignore that my friends are calling him by name too. Something changed at the game Wednesday night, and not just the part where we're suddenly gossip fodder on Page Six. Or the part where my mother's taken up drinking.

Yes, yes, it's watered-down wine coolers, but for Mom, that's like doing vodka shots off an ice luge. She has the shoulders of Norwegian Vikings and the alcohol tolerance of a toddler. Some things, you just can't explain.

Like this irrational wish I'm doing my best to ignore that Chase will show up tonight and watch us play.

So I can torture him what my talented fingers can do.

Yep.

It's all about the torture.

Definitely not about wanting to show off. Wanting him to see me shine.

Wanting him to be impressed.

And, you know, turned on. Going primal, barging onto the stage, tossing the instruments out of his way, throwing me over his shoulder and taking me back to his place where we can bang each other's brains out all night long.

Nope, definitely none of that going on here. That's disgusting. I've seen quite enough of Chase Jett's hard, flexible, sinful body to last a lifetime.

"Five minutes, ladies."

My friends are staring at me.

"Did you invite him?" Eloise asks.

"What? Who? My brothers? No, they'd come galloping up on the stage and steal the show. They're such spotlight hogs."

I get a triple hit of *Don't play dumb, Sia.*

"I'd have to like him to invite him," I grumble.

"Oh, honey," Willow sighs.

Eloise snorts. "Don't lose your place in the set list," she tells me. "I like this place. I'd play here again, but they have to ask us first."

I sling an arm around her shoulder and squeeze. "I love you guys."

I might be unemployed by Tuesday, but I'll always have my band.

16

Chase

I'M SITTING in the back of an Irish bar, drinking a scotch, and watching Bro's all-girl band cover the best boy band songs of the last three decades.

Only in New York. This town fucking rocks.

I forgot she could sing. Her voice is chocolate silk, rich and decadent and wrapping around me like a lover's caress. She could be singing "Itsy Bitsy Spider" for all I care. For this moment, when she doesn't know I'm here, I can soak her up without having to pretend.

Her voice, I might've forgotten, but the piano lessons, I remember. After three years of ear torture, Ares put a fist through the instrument. Told his parents there was a spider and that he was protecting Zeus. Using small words and a few hand gestures, of course. *Lots of legs. Bad bug. Scaredy Zeus.* And then he'd shown everyone his biceps.

It worked. They bought Bro a keyboard with headphones

instead, and everyone's lives were vastly improved. Gotta hand it to her—her keyboard playing is drastically better.

Or all of this could be choreographed and lip-synced.

A week ago, I would've thought it with a superior sneer. Today, I'd be disappointed if she wasn't real.

Not that I'll admit it to her.

I have a half-drunk bottle of cheap white wine—she strikes me as the red type—a bouquet of flowers that I put on my chair and bounced on with my ass, and a box of coconut chocolates on the table. Ambrosia hates coconut like normal people hate expired milk or wasp stings. Probably because she's allergic. If this doesn't say *I hate you, let's go fuck in the back alley*, I'll have to accept the fact that I'll spend the rest of my life at half-mast with no hope of satisfaction.

Which might be preferable to confessing to her that I may not hate her at all.

They've been playing for about forty-five minutes. I'm not sure how long their set goes, but I'm getting antsy. I've had a raging hard-on since I got Zeus's text yesterday telling me about Bro's band. Girl bands are fucking hot, period. Girl bands with Bro in them are *don't look too close or you'll burn your retinas out*.

And I actually *do* mean that in the complimentary way.

They finish up "Bye Bye Bye" and hit the opening chords of some classic New Kids on the Block, and suddenly two overgrown blond apes leap on the stage.

Are you fucking *kidding* me?

I can't get in Bro's pants with her brothers here. And those leggings she's sporting are a fucking wet dream. They're sparkly with a red and black swirly-pattern that highlights every curve and crevice. The short tank that lands just above her belly button isn't bad either, though I'd rather that was my face on her chest than some boy band dude.

On stage, she rolls her eyes, but she's smiling. Willow's

shaking a tambourine in front of the mic with Parker rocking the guitar beside her, both of them laughing. They shift to the side to give the Berger twins more room, and the doofuses—doofusi?—break into boy band dance moves.

I hope Zeus thought to check the structural integrity of the stage before jumping up there.

Willow starts singing with Bro doing backup on "The Right Stuff," and holy *shit*, the stage is literally shaking under the Berger twins.

Not that I care.

Because when Bro's not singing, she's laughing.

Head tipped back, long neck exposed, eyes dancing like pixies in the moonlight. I want to be her keyboard, those fingers tripping over me. I want to be her mic, that voice channeling through me. I want to be her chair.

Because *duh*. Damn fucking right I want her straddling me.

Cut me some slack here. Limited blood flow. Poetry only goes so far when it's been three fucking days since I've been buried inside her tight little pussy.

I want that.

I want her to laugh at *me*. I want her to smile at *me*. I want her to come for *me*.

And I want it *now*.

I grab my gifts, flag down a waiter, and slip him a grand to get me backstage and end their set. Two minutes later, Bro and her band come tripping down the hall.

She freezes when she sees me. "Hello, dickhead," she says hesitantly, like she isn't sure the word tastes right.

I shove the gifts at her. Her lips start to curl as she takes in the crushed flowers, and her brows crash down at the obviously half-empty wine bottle. "The chocolates are filled with coconut," I say. "Let's fuck."

She grabs me by the shirt and hauls me into a small room,

kicks the door shut, and locks it. Her hands are down my pants before I can count to hallelujah. "You look like you slept in horseshit after the horse ate glitter," she says.

I rip her tank off and grab her breasts. *God*, they're bags of hot orgasmic honey wrapped in pink lace that I'm going to suck until she screams my name. "You sing like your vocal chords are made of the rotting corpses of rejected lab frogs."

She's stroking me and squeezing me and licking her lips while I pump in her hand and pray she still has those sharp fingernails and a hatred of my balls, because *Christ*, I need to feel everything—pain, pleasure, passion, *everything*. She pushes me backward, and a set of drums and cymbals clatter to the ground.

"Fucking klutz," she says.

"I'm going to fucking bang you on those drums."

"I'd like to see you try."

"I'll just bet you would."

She drops my cock to grab my face and stick her tongue down my throat, and I squeeze her breasts. She jumps on me, wrapping her legs around my hips, and we stumble backward. My back connects with a wooden shelf. Something that feels like a half-full jug of milk grazes my temple. Bro has my bare cock nestled between her legs, rubbing and grinding and driving me to sweet torture, the fabric on her leggings adding an erotic friction.

Fuck, I've needed this.

I grip her ass and knead it while I yank her tighter against me, making her rock harder against my straining shaft. I'm so hard I'm about to split skin and my balls are so tight I can feel them under my ribs.

So. Fucking. Good.

She punches me in the shoulder. "Shut up, dickwad. We're *not* good."

I lift her ass and bite her nipple. Her head falls back and

she cries out, but when I jerk my mouth away—I'm having twisted sex with a woman who hates me, but I'm not a total asshole—she shoves it back to her breast.

"You fucking animal," she pants. "Try that again like you actually mean it."

I nip again, and she squeezes her thighs so tight around my hips I wonder if it's possible for her legs to crush bones. She's rocking her pussy on just the tip of my dick, and Holy. Fucking. Vixen.

Her legs tighten more, and she's still rocking her hot, wet center on my head while I nip and suck and pull on her nipples. She can probably crush beer cans between her thighs. She squeezes tighter, pumping like a fucking bunny teasing the top of my cock, and I start to lose feeling in my toes.

This woman. God almighty. I want to fuck her on her back, against the wall, in my shower, on my floor, on my kitchen table, on that beanbag chair in her office, facing her, taking her from behind, sixty-nine, on a set of fucking trapeze bars, and then I want to do it all over again.

She's slick and wet, so fucking ready for me. I pull her perfect breasts out of the lace bra and lick a circle around one nipple, then the other, before clenching down again. She has a rock hard grip on my head, holding it there while I feast on the rosy buds.

Her tits taste like her name. *Ambrosia*. Nectar of the gods. Too potent for human consumption.

I'm going to fucking eat her anyway. I'd die of Ambrosia poisoning, and I wouldn't have a single regret.

She's mewling and crying and pumping against my stomach and my head, saying my name.

Chase, Chase, Chase in that hot chocolate wine voice.

And I'd thought she was playing music before.

I shove away from the shelf, trip over the drums, and catch

us before I crush her. There. A desk. I lunge for it and drop her sweet ass on the edge. She leans back on her hands, lifting her ass, and I rip her leggings off. She spreads her long, creamy thighs and silently dares me to touch her. I run a finger under the edge of her pink lace panties. She shivers. She's watching me with hooded eyes, breath coming fast, her fantastic tits rising and falling and distracting me from the promised land.

"Need a map again?" she says, and maybe it's my imagination, but I can't hear the disgust. Like she can't fake it anymore either.

But I know Bro.

If I say something nice, I'm not getting to lick her pussy. I stroke her smooth skin again, just beneath the edge of the teensy triangle, and my cock wants to know why we're not plundering and pillaging already.

She shudders, moans, and drops her head back.

That's why.

I want to see her pleasure. I want to see her lose herself.

I want to know *I* did it to her, and I want her to know it's me.

"I don't know what you think you're doing, but it's boring me," she gasps.

"You probably taste like three-day-old roadkill."

"Your tongue wouldn't know the difference between roadkill and Kobe steak."

I rip the bows on her thong. It falls away, and I bury my face at the apex between her thighs, in that sweet, pink pillow hiding her magic button. I lick her seam, taste her arousal, and plunge my tongue where no man will ever go again.

This is *mine*.

She rocks on my face, my hair fisted in her grip while I lick and suck and nip her clit just like I worshipped her tits.

And if her tits were the nectar of the gods, her creamy center is the forbidden fruit. My balls are so tight dots are dancing in my vision. My dick is pulsing so hard it has its own heartbeat, chanting *mine, mine, mine.*

Her thighs clench around my ears. She cries out my name, and the heady taste of her orgasm coats my tongue. I lap it up, her body pulsing and writhing around my face while she yanks my hair out by the roots, coming and coming and coming.

Just when I think she's done, I squeeze a finger into her pussy.

She clenches around me and her breath comes out on a wheezy cry.

I add another finger, then a third, thrusting, rubbing, searching. She pumps against my hand.

I nip her clit again, and *god*, wave after wave of spasms squeeze my fingers until they're numb.

"Holy *fuck*," she gasps.

I rise on shaky legs. My cock is so engorged I might've strained something vital in it. "Was that good for you?" I push at her entrance with my dick, watching my head slide along the seam of her bare pussy.

She shoves a strand of hair out of her face. "You're still here?" she pants. "I barely noticed."

I press deeper, her walls so fucking hot and wet and tight, I wonder if maybe she couldn't crush a beer can with her vagina too.

"You can't feel *that*?" I smirk. I know she can, and she knows I know she can.

"You mean your crinkly winky?" she fires back.

I thrust my *crinkly winky* deeper into her core.

She gasps and rides it, the sight of her sweet, milky pussy riding my dick making me impossibly harder.

"That little crooked pencil?" she moans. She grips my tight balls and rakes her nails over them, and *oh baby, yes*.

I sheath myself all the way up to the hilt. One thrust. Two. I have my dick buried so far inside her I might never get it all back out. I don't *want* to come out. I want to let her ride my rocket until we're both blind, but she's so fucking hot, I can barely hold back.

Chase Jett is not a three-thrust wonder.

Just for the record.

With superhuman strength, I pull myself almost all the way out. "If you don't appreciate my giant, oversized, novelty *pencil*, then maybe I'll go put it in another pencil box."

She sinks her nails into my ass and tries to tug me back in. I thrust at the edges of her pussy, teasing her with my head, but I don't give her what she wants.

She's jerking against me, inching closer, riding higher up on my dick, and it's pissed at me too. *Let's just bang the hot pussy. I'm not fucking Superman.*

I can still taste her, and I know she's going to squeeze me dry when I finally let her. But once I let go, it's over. She'll kick my ass out of the room, pretend she doesn't know me, and we'll have to do this dance again before I get through her pearly gates once more.

She shuts her eyes, drops her head back, rubs her hands over her breasts, teasing her own nipples, which sets off fireworks in my gut and nearly overrides my self-control. She's fucking touching herself, and it's the hottest thing I've ever seen.

And then she does the one thing that I don't and can't anticipate.

"*Please*, Chase," she whimpers.

How the *fuck* can I resist that?

I shove into her like I'm coming home. My cock is doing the driving, thrusting, grinding, pumping, into her hot, wet, silky pussy. She's already pulsing around me, aftershocks from her first two trips up the mountain or precursors to the real show, I don't know. All I know is I'm buried up to my balls in Bro's slick pussy, she's raking her nails over my back, thrusting her tongue in my mouth, biting my lip, and matching me thrust for thrust like I'm her salvation.

The metal desk bangs on the wall. A mug of pencils clatters to the ground. She clenches around my shaft and buries her claws in my ass, and I'm done. I come like a rocket, firing deep inside her while she spasms and screams and comes all over me again.

I ride wave after wave after wave of release, every pulse, every heartbeat, every explosion and aftershock making up for not having her in my bed every minute of the last three days. My legs give out as I spend my last, and I collapse on top of her on the desk.

Her fingers rest in my hair. Her heart pounds in my ear, and her breasts pillow my head.

She doesn't push me away.

God in heaven, if she thinks we're going again, I'm going to need an hour.

My joystick is still buried inside her. At the idea of another round, it twitches and lifts an interested ear.

"You have *got* to be kidding me," Bro murmurs. "Some of us have to walk tomorrow."

I smile against her skin.

She just said something nice to me. Not that I plan on letting her know I noticed.

The room slowly comes back into focus. Drums all over. A stool upended too. A sheaf of papers got scattered. There's a bottle of bleach on its side in front of the shelves, Bro's clothes scattered about. I'm somehow still wearing my shirt.

And my pants.

My dick was free, so that was enough.

Next time, we're doing this in a bed. Or I might have to trick her into trying that top-of-the-Empire-State-Building thing with the pile of hundred dollar bills first.

She might need more public sex before she's comfortable at my place. Or before she'd let me back into her place. I grew up in a two-bedroom shack. I'm not picky. Though her neighbors were oddly disturbing. Definitely my place first.

I suddenly freeze. "Are there fucking cameras in here?"

She laughs, and my cock swells inside her. She wiggles, and more blood channels back into my dick.

"Didn't you read the warning on the bottle of those little blue pills?" she says.

I twist my head and bite her nipple.

She clenches around my dick. I'm sore and spent and wobbly, but I rock inside her anyway. Because she's not kicking me out. She's not leaving me.

"Seriously, do dick enhancements come with the fortune?" she says.

I'm at full-mast, and I'm already where I want to be. I suck her nipple all the way to the back of my throat, and she arches into me, grinding against my over stimulated woody. Once she's worked up, panting and writhing and pulling my hair and humping me like a rabbit, I let her breast go, scraping my teeth along the hard little bud.

"Where do you think I got my fortune?" I murmur.

"Money laundering," she grits out.

"I think you'd like to have a thick, long roll of my money right where my dick is," I say.

Her hips jerk. "Oh my god," she moans.

"I'd like to watch you ride a chilled bottle of thousand-dollar champagne."

She's picturing it. I can tell by the way her eyes go distant and her hips can't keep a steady rhythm.

"And then I'll drink it out of your pussy," I add.

She explodes around me again, and my cock tries to match her volcanic release, but I don't have anything left to give. I just ride on the aftershocks, letting her milk me with her core until she's limp. Her breathing is shallow, her eyes have rolled back in her head, and for half a second, I wonder if we've actually killed her.

"You," she rasps out, "are a dirty, dirty man."

She likes it. For her, I'll be the filthiest fucker to ever walk the planet. "You have no idea, princess."

For the first time in my life, I'm wrapped in a comfortable silence with Bro.

So *this* is what it feels like to not hate her.

Or possibly to like her.

Or possibly more than like her.

I'm half-hunched on her, still sheathed in her warm center. She's crooked on the desk, eyes still closed, with what looks like the makings of a good neck cramp with the way her head's leaning against the wall.

But it's the soft, quiet realness of her that gets to me.

I've never seen her not fighting.

I run a hand down her arm, and a smile teases her lips. It's subtle, but it's there. I'm risking my balls staying attached to my body now, and I know it, but I squeeze her in a gentle hug.

She squeezes back—lightly enough she could claim it was a twitch if she wanted to—and my heart melts.

I'm done, ladies and gentlemen. Bro Berger won a gold medal in the orgasm Olympics, and now she's hugging me. On purpose.

I turn my head and press a kiss between her breasts. "How did you like Vassar?" I say.

She goes from chill to shrieking harpy in under a second. Her fist catches my shoulder, and she uses both her feet to shove me away. My dick flops cold and wet against my thigh.

111

"*Get out*," she screeches. She leaps upright, fully naked, a flush covering her entire body. "*Get. The. Fuck. Out. Now.*"

I hold up a hand. "Whoa, hey, I—"

A drumstick flies at my head. Then a mug. She grabs a printer cartridge from the shelf, and I duck that too.

"Bro, calm down, I—"

"Don't—" Where did that shoe come from? "—ever—" Oh, Christ, the jug of bleach too "—talk—" A stone Buddha head? Are you *kidding*? We're in an *Irish bar*. "—to me—" *Fuck*, that's a full bottle of Jameson "—*again*."

Running away is not in my DNA. Despite what Bro might tell you about the night we screwed around in the giant bratwurst on wheels, I don't run.

I make tactical decisions based on my circumstances.

And I know, without a doubt, that leaving this woman to wreck this office in peace is my smartest course of action.

I'll leave a few big bills with management to cover the damages and call her tomorrow. But right now, I'm not letting the door hit me on my ass on the way out.

17

Ambrosia

I AM the world's biggest sucker. Is it possible to be completely and utterly satisfied down to your marrow and so freaking enraged you want to go all Incredible Hulk on every penis on the face of the planet? Just want to bend them all until they snap in two?

Ah, I'm asking for a friend.

Because of course I wasn't stupid enough to think sex with Chase Jett and his magic peen could come without a price.

I hurl one last potato at the closed door and sink to my knees in the carnage of the supply-slash-prep room.

Afterglow gone. I'm achingly empty and hollow inside. I come from a good family. I'm moderately intelligent. Still young and pretty enough to attract normal, decent men, yet here I am, sexed-up and slapped down by the one man who has tortured me my entire life.

And I keep letting him in.

What the hell is wrong with me?

The door opens, and Zeus peeks in. "Hey, sis, what—whoa! *DUDE*. My eyeballs. Frozen Moses on a popsicle stick, *my eyeballs.*"

I fire a drumstick at him and miss.

He's four freaking feet wide, almost seven feet tall, with his fists shoved into his eye sockets so he's basically blind, and I freaking *miss*. I try again with a potato from the bag I found under the desk. The desk where Chase just made me come so hard I think I might've found some other woman's orgasm at the same time. Is that a thing? Cosmic orgasm-borrowing?

Sign me up for a donation. I don't need mine anymore. I'll give back the one I borrowed and offer up all of mine to someone who's missing hers.

The potato bounces off the wall beside Zeus, missing by a country mile.

I am such a freaking failure.

"Get out," I say, but I can't find the heat. It's just gone.

Like me.

I'm gone. I don't know me anymore. Who is this woman who has possessed my body, and when can I have my regularly scheduled life back?

"Get dressed or I'm sending Ares in," Zeus huffs. "And clean up some of this shit. The manager's going to have a shit fit." The door slams, and it occurs to me that my brothers just stood guard while I had a booty call that, by the looks of this room, was pretty damn acrobatic.

I either have the best brothers in the world, or we're all highly disturbed and need family counseling.

Or possibly both.

18

Ambrosia

I DON'T REMEMBER GETTING home. After the last twenty-four hours, I'm lucky I can remember my name. I think it's been twenty-four hours.

Life is a little hazy.

There's fading light outside my apartment window. It must be dusk. I say that, but I'm not actually sure I saw light earlier either. I probably did, because none of the lamps are on in my apartment, and I don't think we've been sitting in the dark for hours.

Willow, Parker, Eloise, and I are doing a real-life experiment testing hangover cures. Above me, Hogzilla is once again demonstrating that she's better at relationships than I am.

She's probably also better at avoiding getting arrested.

Fucking Chase Jett.

Yes, *fucking Chase Jett* is, once again, the dumbest thing I've ever done.

I pour a round of organic, fair trade, responsibly-harvested mango orange guava juice from Whole Foods—take *that*, Dickhead—into mason jars and pass them around. We all lift our glasses. "To the Dick List," we say in unison.

Hogzilla's bedsprings give an ominously long, loud creak, and I say a prayer that whoever she's humping tonight isn't the size of a house. I don't want Hogzilla and her boy toy—boy toys?—to come crashing through the ceiling.

Oh, hardy har. *Come* crashing. Interpret that as you may.

Speaking of men the size of houses, my brothers, annoying overgrown ape-men that they are, were my unlikely heroes last night. I don't know what they told the manager or the cops after Zeus ordered me back into my clothes, and I frankly don't care. I will never say another bad thing about them as long as I live. They got me out of another trip to the slammer and offered to pay for all the damages.

And because they're my brothers and they can't help themselves, they also bought every last bottle of alcohol in the bar, tipped the bartender some obscene amount of money, rented a limo, and got me and my friends shit-faced while we toured the city.

My memories of this weekend pretty much consist of Before The Question and The Aftermath.

Before he dropped his little *gotcha* question?

Four orgasms. Enough said. Maybe I would've said more had The Question not happened, but it did, and I'll always have my four orgasms to remember.

The Aftermath is really hazy. And not because of the alcohol.

I don't want to talk about it.

Let's just say I've come to realize I did something even more stupid than letting him have free reign to my vagina without a condom again. This is what distance and perspective have given me.

"Where *is* the Dick List?" Eloise says. "I need to add someone."

I grab my phone to open the list, only wincing a little at the name taunting me from the top.

Walking hasn't exactly been a stroll in the park today, and I don't regret that nearly as much as I want to.

He gave me *four fucking orgasms*, okay? It's like being sorry my hoo-ha got high. Would I do it again? No. But knowledge is power, people. I now have the four-orgasm knowledge.

"Name?" I ask Eloise.

She blushes.

Eloise blushes.

"Just give me the fucking phone and don't ask any questions," she says.

I gasp. "You're putting one of my brothers on the list."

"I said no questions." She swings her finger around the room. "Circle of trust. We don't judge the Dick List."

"Can anyone ever fall off the list?" Willow asks.

Parker hits her with my stuffed elephant that I won at Coney Island three years ago. "Not the time," she hisses.

"I'm not talking about *him*," she replies. "But sometimes good people make mistakes."

"For the last time, we are *not* taking your landlord off the list."

"He can stay. He told me I was *taking a tone* about my fridge being broken last week." For a woman with royal relatives, Willow puts up with a lot of shit. "I'm planning a wedding. I have liberty to take as many tones as I want with as many people as I want. Plus, *the fridge is broken*."

For Willow, this is the same as renting a horse and carriage solely to ride around standing up and flipping off all of Central Park.

Parker doesn't care that she's having a meltdown though. "Then who?"

Willow goes pink. "It was a hypothetical question."

Eloise is taking entirely too long to put a single name on the list, and I need that list, because I want to know who else on the list Willow might be thinking about taking off it. We use first names only in case the list ever ends up in the wrong hands—a precaution I'm exceptionally grateful for after this last week—but we all know who most of the guys are.

"Did one of my exes make a pass at you?" Parker demands.

"Never mind," Willow says. "Once a dick, always a dick. My head hurts. Are we trying coffee yet?"

I steal the phone back from Eloise and find *both* of my brothers on the list. "Are you *kidding* me?" I squeak. "*Both* of them."

"*Circle of trust.*" Eloise scowls at me. "And for all you know, I met two other guys with the same names as your brothers last night."

"She's mad that Ares wouldn't sleep with her, and Zeus wouldn't be used to make Ares jealous," Parker tells me.

"You can't put my brothers on the Dick List for that," I tell Eloise. "It's my fault. I know too many stories that could ruin their reputations, and they know I'll use them if I have to."

"I heard Zeus telling Ares that Chase has a lot of work to do if he's ever going to win you over," Willow says.

For the innocent one in the group, she's quite devious. "You did not," I say.

She shrugs and heads for the coffee pot. "They love you. They love him. They think if you love each other, they get the best of everything."

I open my mouth to argue, but she has a valid point.

The twins lost their best friend after the Bratwurst Wagon incident. *I* was sure they were better off without him,

I never stopped to consider what it would mean to them if the two of us could get along.

I still let their names stay on the Dick List though.

Parker's phone dings. She glances at it, and her mouth forms a perfect O. "Get out!" she says, thumbs flying over the screen.

"What? *What?*" We all circle around her.

"We made Page Six," she gasps. "Our band made Page Six!"

Oh. My. God.

There we are, the four of us plus my brothers, right in the center of New York's biggest gossip page.

"What does it say?" Willow squeals.

I groan and cover my eyes. "I don't want to know what it says."

"Amateur band, okay, we can take that," Parker murmurs, "decent vocals—*nice*, Willow, and they don't even mention your stepdad—*crowd loved us!* They say the crowd loved us!"

"They say the crowd loved the Twin Tanks Right-Stuffing it," Eloise grumbles. "Damn yahoos can't *right stuff* anything."

Parker snorts, then all three of them go eerily quiet while they stare at the phone.

"How bad is it?" I whisper.

"Not bad," Parker says quickly. "Really. Just gossip pages being gossip pages."

So, basically, I can never show my face at work again. Or anywhere else in the city. Chase is new money, but he's money. It doesn't matter. He screwed me in an elevator, dry-humped me on a Kiss Cam, and now the whole world knows I trashed a supply closet after screwing his brains out in there too.

"It's just conjecture that you hooked up," Willow flits back to the coffee pot and digs my only two clean mugs out of my cabinets. "They don't even mention the police being called."

"It could be a lot worse," Parker adds.

"Far worse for him than you," Eloise assures me. "No one thinks you're in love with him."

I grab Parker's phone, enlarge the font, and scroll through.

They're right.

No mention of the cops. No mention of my temper tantrum. Not even a hint that we did the dirty deed in the back of the bar.

Just a side picture of Chase and his broody, hungry, determined eyes trained on something.

My belly drops.

Because I don't know what I'm seeing, and I don't want to care, but I can't help myself.

Either they're right, and he *wants* me, or they're dead wrong, and he wants to obliterate me.

Not that there's much difference between the two.

I can't *like* Chase Jett.

I don't know how.

And I'm afraid wanting to just might destroy me.

19

Chase

Saturday morning started at four AM with a flaming bag of dog crap exploding on my front steps. I don't know if it was Bro or her brothers, but I get the message.

I'm persona non grata with the Bergers.

I spent the morning hitting the shit out of a punching bag and the afternoon working. As I'm sitting in the car on the way home, I'm hoping they spray-painted dicks all over my house or hid stink bombs in my bushes or that the overgrown man-children are waiting for me, looking to avenge their womenfolk again.

No such luck.

It's like they don't care enough to acknowledge my existence.

As though I'm a nobody.

My fists clench.

I'm not a fucking nobody. Not anymore.

I head inside and pound on my punching bag until it

splits, but my mind won't shut up and my dick's asking why we're sitting here alone when we could be out pushing Bro's buttons.

I jack off in a cold shower with images of Bro's pussy dancing in my head and the taste of her nipples an elusive memory on my tongue, down three shots of whiskey, and try to sleep.

Somewhere in the middle of the night, I wonder where Bro is. If she's awake. If her upstairs neighbors are having an animal orgy jamboree. If she's thinking about me.

If she's wanting to touch me.

I roll over and pound my pillow, and feathers explode all over my room.

Two weeks ago, I was in California brokering a quarter-billion-dollar deal with the largest internet gaming company in the world. I was in control of my life. In control of my business. In control of my dick.

This week, I fired everyone who knew anything about management at the company I've been positioning myself to buy for three years, because they insulted a woman.

A woman I've despised most of my life.

A woman I can't get out of my head.

By Sunday morning, I can't take it any longer. I call my car around and give the driver Bro's address.

I tell myself I'm not going to touch her. We're just going to talk. My dick smirks. He doesn't believe me.

Her apartment door is painted turquoise. It's a rectangular ocean in a sea of dingy, cracked, dirty sand-colored walls. I knock, and after a moment, it flings open.

"Hey, I've got your phone—" she starts, then her dark eyes land on me and narrow to suspicious little slits. "*You.*"

My *joy sausage* misses the tone and stands up and salutes her. *Oh, yeah, baby, it's me. Come to papa.*

I blow out a slow breath and tell it to picture my grandma naked.

"We need to talk," I say to Ambrosia.

She tries to slam the door, but it's easy to anticipate. I'm halfway inside before the wood bangs into my knee. "Please," I add.

She lifts her fingers in an X like she's warding off evil. "Back, glittery sex demon. I'm exorcising you."

I shove my hands in my pants and wish I was mature enough to pull off a *grow up* look, but she might be onto something. Being possessed would explain this week.

Plus, I can't get the fucking glitter out, and somehow it's spread to every last pair of pants I own. I really do have a glittery crotch.

"I'm not here to take your clothes off," I say, but as the words leave my mouth, all my dick hears is *take your clothes off*, and it leaps in agreement.

Of course, she notices.

I could be in steel-plated armor and she'd notice. She has some kind of internal erection detection system. I can tell by the way her eyes go dark and the way that delicious pink tongue darts out to lick her lush lips while she moves her arms to aim her crossed fingers at my crotch.

He can tell she sees him too. He's trying to wave at her.

Does she have to be so fucking *hot* when she's pissed?

"Back away, and neither one of us will get hurt," she growls.

"Can we pretend to be adults for two minutes and have a simple conversation?" I say.

"You're not a grown-up. You're some kind of male sex kitten in a glitter suit, and I'm done with you."

"I was thinking dinner. In Central Park."

"I am not sucking your dick in Central Park."

"I don't want you to suck my dick. I want you to have dinner with me."

"And eat you," she accuses.

I wish I could say she doesn't look like she'd enjoy going down on me, but I know the signs of rampant lust, and she's waving them like a flag.

Dilated pupils, check. Shallow breathing, check. A barrage of denials and commentary on my junk, check.

It's Bro. She'd tackle me in the produce aisle, rip my pants off, ride me like a donkey, and ask if me that was a microscopic needle in my pants or if the nice scientists in the asylum had noticed I was missing yet.

It's not easy resisting the challenge—my joystick *has* noticed it hasn't yet become intimately acquainted with her mouth, and there's only so much I can do to convince it that it's not in charge here—but I keep my voice level and don't break eye contact. "You can eat vegetarian lasagna for all I care."

"Eggplant lasagna?" Dammit, this woman can make *vegetarian lasagna* filthy. She's so fucking perfect. She cocks a hip. "Carrot lasagna? *Banana* lasagna?"

She's doing it again. She's making my balls ache and my dick do battle with my zipper. "Anything you can get on the printed menu delivered from the kitchen and prepared by the chef," I grind out. "With our clothes on and our hands above the table. I just want to talk. Like normal human beings. Maybe I'll bring flowers. Maybe you'll say thank you."

"I don't know what kind of backwards psychological trick this is, but it won't work. You can't have my pussy. It's closed. Permanently. Zipped up and tossed out in the trash."

My dick sees her throw down and raises her a triple orgasm. "Ambrosia—"

"Do. Not. Call. Me. That."

Staying calm is a battle. Staying unaroused is impossible. "What do you want me to call you?"

"Nothing."

Okay, Nothing, can we talk before we fuck again?

I know I didn't say it out loud, but her eyes shift into pissed-off kitten slits, her fingers twist into gnarled claws, her back hunches, and she hisses a demonic oath at me.

Fine, she stayed human. But I still swear she read my mind.

But you want to know the dumbest part of all of this?

I'm hard as a lead pipe. I know if I just tell her she's a douche-fucker she'll ride me like a stallion until I'm permanently cross-eyed, and all I can think about is that I've never kissed her.

Yeah, I've had my tongue down her throat. We've played tonsil hockey. I know how firm her lip is between my teeth and how far it'll stretch when I pull. I know she tastes like honey and that she can do things with her tongue that are illegal in four states, but I've never kissed her hello.

Or goodbye.

Or *I missed you. How was your day? Steak, chicken, or lamb?*

And I have this ridiculous fucking *need* to kiss her.

The door across the hallway opens. "Is that the boy you banged at the Yankees game?" the old lady asks.

"He tried, but he has a limp dick," Bro replies.

"Too bad. He's a looker. Honey, I don't mind 'em a little limp. You can come try it with me when you get bored with her." She goes back in her apartment, but I get the feeling she's watching us through her peep hole.

Also? Bro just called me a limp dick. I might still have a chance of getting through to her. My dick's cheering—it knows what's up.

Besides it.

"I like you," I grind out.

She goes pale and blinks. She's got the wide-legged stance, hands balled into fists, but she's missing the flash in her eyes. And instead, there's something I can relate to all too well.

Raw, unbidden vulnerability.

Easy to recognize. Same thing's making up ninety percent of my blood right now.

"Are you that desperate to get back in my pants?" Her voice wobbles. Not the breathy, *let's fight and fuck* wobble. The *don't hurt me* wobble.

I angle further into her apartment, leaving my foot in the door so we're not trapped.

It's as much for my sanity as her comfort. I swallow hard. "You're very pretty when you smile."

She starts to sneer, but seems to realize I'm serious. "We have absolutely *nothing* in common."

"We both know where to hit Ares to make him cry like a baby."

"We have nothing *healthy* in common."

"We both like it when you come."

She shoves me in the shoulder. That simple touch lights me up like Times Square at Christmas and sends half my brain power shooting to my dick. I grit my teeth and press on. "You're smart. You're funny. And I can't stop thinking about you."

"Why are you doing this?" she whispers.

She's so close, I could twine my fingers with hers. I could brush her cheek with my thumb. I could tangle my hands in her wavy hair.

I could capture her parted lips and kiss her. Not like the guy who wants to fuck her brains out—we'll get there, because I still want that too—but as the guy who wants to not hate her.

Her eyes are dark as night, dwelling in shadows and

demons and fears. Someone hurt her. Someone hurt her badly.

I suspect that someone was me.

"You're fucking hot." I angle one hip closer to her, still keeping one foot in the door. "I can't stop thinking about your ass. Your tits. Your pussy. And I also can't stop thinking about this smart mouth. Your quick wit. Your balls."

"I don't have balls, you fucking nimwit."

I tuck a strand of hair behind her ear. *Christ*, I want to suck on the soft flesh of her neck and brand her. "You're strong and stubborn and brave, and it makes me so hot I want to rip your clothes off and make you come in my mouth."

"You don't get to say nice things to me." Her eyes squeeze shut. She's shaking. I'm not touching her, but I can feel her shaking.

Or maybe that's me. "What if we could?" I murmur. "What if we could forget yesterday? We're fucking good in bed. What if we're good everywhere?"

"We've never done it in a bed."

"Let me take you to dinner and back to my place. I have six beds. We'll try them all."

Her fingers are inching down my chest, and my cock is straining to meet her path. I'm losing the battle of wills with my body, and having her breasts pressed against me while she angles her face to mine isn't helping. I let myself caress her cheeks, soft as peaches, and trace her lush lips.

Squeak...squeak...squeak...

"Afraid of hogzilla?" She whispers. "You're such a pussy."

"Say something nice, and I'll eat your pussy before we go to dinner."

"You'd like that, wouldn't you?"

"I would." Being honest with her is the single fucking

hardest thing I've done in my life. "I'd very much like eating your pussy."

"You're lying," she grits out while she grinds her palm over the denim trapping my shaft.

I want to rock into her touch, but instead I push her hand away. My cock howls in protest. "One nice thing, and we both get what we want."

She battles me and goes for the button on my jeans. "Quit fucking around and just do me."

Oh, how I want to. "I like it when you give orders."

Her fingers still, but she still won't look at me.

"You remember that time you smeared *I let my dog do me up the ass* on my old Ford? That was so fucking hot. I couldn't stop thinking about you thinking about my ass."

"I like your ass," she whispers.

Oh, thank Christ. I cup her breasts and flick my thumbs over her nipples poking through her shirt. "I like your breasts."

"I like your ugly chin dimple."

Close enough. I nip lightly on her neck. "I like the way you grip my hair when you're coming."

She's fumbling with my zipper. "I like that thing you do with your tongue."

"Which thing?"

"All the things." My rod finally springs free, and she gives it a long, sure stroke from balls to tip and back again.

"Can we shut the door?" I hiss out.

She yanks on my dick to guide me all the way into her apartment. The door slams shut. Bedsprings squeak overhead.

She sinks her upper teeth into her lower lip and hits me with wide, vulnerable eyes. "I like your arms," she whispers while she strokes me again.

She's not trying to strangle me, but her touch is making

me impossibly hard. My cock strains in her hand, and I can't stop my hips from jerking into her touch. "You have amazing fingers," I tell her.

"I like your penis."

"It likes you too."

She bends to get a closer look, and *fuck*, then she's licking my tip, swirling her lithe, pink tongue around me while she cradles my balls.

I'm holding on by a thread, because if I thought hate-fucking her brains out was mind-bending, having her lush lips wrapped around my cock, her mouth sliding over me while her tongue suckles me like a lover is taking euphoria to another plane of existence.

"Holy fuck, Bro." I grip her hair while she settles on her knees and takes me deeper. My legs are shaking. My heart's about to give out. And my shaft is begging for more.

She moans as she takes me all the way in, her eyes sliding back into her head, her fingers kneading my tight balls, her tongue swirling and gliding against me like I'm the most delicious fucking thing she's ever had in her mouth, and everything goes white. My hips jerk out of control. She's sucking and licking and rubbing and I'm throbbing harder and longer and thicker than I've ever been before, and if I start coming, I won't stop. I try to pull out. "Ambrosia—" I gasp.

She sinks those perfect nails into my ass and takes me impossibly deeper down her hot, wet throat, her tongue still worshipping me, her teeth scraping my flesh, and I can't hold back any longer. I come down her throat, a roar erupting from my soul while I pound into her mouth and she drinks me up, every last tremor cradled on her tongue, every surge met with a suck, until she's satisfied and I can barely stand.

Rainbow stars are blurring my vision. When she releases

me with a *pop*, she presses kisses along the length of my still-hard dick. "Good boy," she croons.

I drop to my knees, and not just because they can't hold me anymore. She's wearing a smug, satisfied smile, but her dark eyes tell me she's not nearly done.

Good, because I'm not done with her.

"Good girl," I say. "Now tell me you'll go to dinner with me."

She's toying with the buttons on my shirt. "If I don't?" she pants.

I cup her pussy and find her leggings hot and soaked. She arches into my touch, and I grind my palm against her. She thrusts into my hand.

"Say you'll go to dinner with me, or I'll quit touching you." I kiss her before she can say something we'll both regret, but this isn't our usual kiss.

This kiss is slow and leisurely. I'm not plundering, I'm exploring. I'm not gripping her hair, I'm letting my fingers tangle in the silky strands the way I want her tangled in my sheets. I can taste me in her mouth, and it makes my dick throb again. I rock against her, not to get off, but to show her what she does to me.

"I want to touch you," I whisper against her mouth.

"I—I need you to touch me," she whispers back.

And just like that, I'm lost.

Game over. I'm done.

My soul will forever belong to Ambrosia May Berger. Everything else be damned.

20

Ambrosia

CHASE SHOULDN'T BE HERE. I shouldn't have given him head, and I shouldn't agree to go to dinner with him.

But I *want* to. I *need* to.

I crave him like an addict craves drugs, and I don't want to quit.

He slides his hand into my pants, his strong, sure fingers easily finding their way in my playground. I tug my leggings down to give him easier access, and I spread my legs like the wanton sex goddess I want to be.

All the while, he's kissing me. Gliding his tongue into my mouth as though we have all the time in the world, stroking my tongue with his, coaxing my lips to open wider instead of just taking what he wants.

This is different.

It's new.

And it's making me ache deep in my core like I've never

ached before. As though it's not just my body that craves his touch, but also a part of my soul.

This is dangerous.

He slides a single finger up inside me, where I'm hot and slick and ready, and I arch into him. Not fast—there's a slow spiral building deep inside me, and it's hard and aching and desperate, but *good*. So damn good.

He's delicious. His tongue, his mouth, his cock—all perfect. I want to suck on his fingers. I want to bite his earlobes. I want to shove him on his back and sink onto his hard, curved length.

"I like how sexy you are," he tells my neck.

His thumb finds my clit, and I pump into his touch. Even when he's being a gentleman, he makes me wild and carnal and more than a little unhinged.

"I like how you like me," I gasp.

He chuckles.

I like his chuckle. It's music.

It shouldn't be—I don't know if this is truly a truce, if he somehow *didn't* know about everything that happened ten years ago, or if he hates me beyond all reason and is a master psychopath, but I can't help myself.

He knows how to play me, and I'm helpless to resist.

"You taste like your name," he tells my nipples.

And I giggle.

Lord help me, Chase Jett is making me giggle while he finger-fucks me.

"My nipples like you," I say.

He rewards my good behavior by sucking and biting said nipples until I'm a writhing jellyfish of lust, pumping and thrusting against his hand until I explode in a million little satisfied pieces. And while the world spins, and the hogzilla mating call filters through the ceiling, and my whole body rides my afterglow, he strokes my arm and kisses and licks a leisurely trail from my breasts to my ear.

"You're a fucking goddess," he tells me.

"My mother almost named me Hera," I murmur in my satisfied haze. "But she didn't like the incestuous implications."

His hand slows, and I realize he's shaking with silent laughter. "Your family is fucking nuts," he says.

And honestly?

It really is the nicest thing he's said to me all day.

Because we are, and only someone as twisted as all of us could fully appreciate it the way I know Chase does.

21

Ambrosia

I TEST this newfound *niceness* between us by complimenting his finger skills, which leads to him having an early dinner between my legs. We both get off while we're supposed to be showering, and then I let Chase take me to dinner where we discuss the possibilities of world domination if we were to actually combine our powers of evil for the ultimate use of good.

It's weird to consider Chase a teammate, but together, we could top any pranks Zeus and Ares could ever dream up. And not just because he can afford like a thousand times better prank equipment.

Also, when Chase and I are nice to each other, we actually have more sex.

Regularly. At least, so far this afternoon, that seems to be the case.

And it's fucking awesome.

Who knew?

"I don't know if I can completely not hate you," I tell him over dessert, which he insisted we had to get, because he's a masochistic bastard who thinks that waiting another hour to jump each other's bones again will somehow make us better people.

His eyes glaze over, and next thing I know, he's hustling me into the backseat of a fancy car with a roll-up partition. "Home," he tells the driver, then he puts the partition up and attacks me like a rabid bunny. "Tell me I have a crooked dick," he growls.

"It's so twisted it belongs in a mental hospital," I say.

He grins and dives for my pussy. "Yeah, baby, my dick and I can both live with you and that ugly mouth."

And that's the last time he makes me come in public for the rest of the day.

But at his place?

I don't know. I lost count.

22

Ambrosia

WORK FEELS WEIRD MONDAY MORNING. And not just because I'm ridiculously, wonderfully sore in all the places I'm not supposed to talk about at work, or because I spent the majority of Sunday having wild monkey sex with the boss.

After hating Chase most of my life, liking him—and admitting it—has me off-kilter.

Maybe we're going too fast. Maybe we're delusional.

Maybe there's a part of me terrified that he's still playing me.

Whatever the case, I didn't think about the Bratwurst Wagon or Vassar for most of the day, and I'm working on convincing myself that I can forgive and forget.

My body has.

My mind isn't completely on board.

Probably because it's the rational, logical part of me pointing out that while sex is great—and more of it with a sex god like Chase is even better—we have a history we're ignoring in favor of setting new boinking records.

Thankfully, things are almost normal in the office. Madison and April and I have a brainstorming meeting where we discuss fall vegetables, spicing up chicken, and a local cheese campaign. If anyone's still whispering about my sex life, they're being subtle enough that I don't notice. April mentioned seeing the write-up about our band and my brothers on Page Six, but didn't mention Chase at all.

My favorite snack bar lady let me pay for my own lunch —though she did offer a wink and insisted on sliding me a protein bar—and now it's nearly four, and I'm positive things here are getting back to normal.

Excluding the forty-seven times an hour that I've wondered if Chase was in the building, or if he was thinking about me, or if he was serious about that thing with the Empire State Building and the bottle of champagne and the blindfold, or if he's been barely resisting coming down here—heh, *coming* —to clear the floor out and make it our personal sex room.

I'm debating the wisdom of sending him a dirty text asking when he's getting off tonight—*heh*, getting off—when Madison suddenly says, "Whoa." She's standing by the window, peering down and groping for her camera. "I haven't seen that since I was a kid."

April pops up next to her. "Oh my god!" she squeals. "The Bratwurst Wagon!"

Every cell in my body goes into full-on catatonic seizure.

The.

Bratwurst.

Wagon.

I hold my breath. It's just driving by. Thirty seconds from now, this will be a distant memory, forever suppressed by my coping mechanisms. It's a coincidence. It's an evil trick of the light. It's not Chase pulling the ultimate prank by proving that he not only has all the money and power, he also has my pussy wrapped around his balls.

"Why's it parked in front of the building?" Madison says.

"Maybe Mr. Jett's buying us all dinner," April suggests. "Remember last week, he sent us all bratwurst for lunch?"

Parker's at my side, shoving my head between my knees, which is really awkward in a beanbag chair. "Breathe, Sia, breathe," she whispers.

My phone dings.

I fumble for it, and see a message from Chase. *Got you a surprise. Look outside.*

Oh, no, he didn't.

But I make myself climb to my feet, cross the room, and stare out the window.

There it is. Twenty feet of brown, wrinkled bratwurst and tan bun on wheels, parked right there under my window.

The bratwurst is taunting me. And so is—

"That fucking douche-shit," I gasp.

"Okay, honey, that's not a thing." Parker's using that soothing voice moms use to calm irrational overtired toddlers. She wraps an arm around me and steers me away from the window. "I'm sure it's a mistake. You know we don't let non-organic bratwurst in the building."

Logically, I know she's right.

But *he fucking brought up Vassar.*

Then he fucked my brains out.

He pretended he liked me.

And then he *got me a surprise.*

Why would he stop there? Why not call in the Bratwurst Wagon? Maybe he's bought the whole fucking fleet and he's converting them to Crunchymobiles. Does the restraining order still hold if it's the same bratwurst in a different bun?

"Sia, *stop talking*," Parker hisses.

I'm talking? Oh my god, I'm babbling. I slap my hand over my mouth, but then I can't breathe.

"What's she talking about?" Madison whispers.

"Is she crazy?"

"It's just the Bratwurst Wagon."

"Chase Jett fucked me in the Bratwurst Wagon," I blurt.

Parker tugs me toward the door. "She had some bad shrimp at lunch," she tells our coworkers.

"I did *not*." I shake her off. "He took my virginity on the floor between the cabinets where they store the buns and the fridge where they keep the sausages. And then the cops showed up, and he told me to drive and he ran like a lily-livered dog turd, and I got arrested for stealing a giant bratwurst on wheels while he got to be a billionaire." I fling a finger at the window. *"And now he's taunting me."*

Every last one of my coworkers is staring at me like I'm two buns short of a pack. Like I got some sausage and now I've lost my marbles.

The hot prick of tears stabs me in the eyeballs, and I'm mortified to realize I'm about to cry.

Over a Bratwurst Wagon.

And Chase Jett.

And I'm not sure which one makes me more mad.

I grab my purse and storm out. I need to call my brothers. I need air.

I need to use the back exit so I don't break my fucking restraining order.

And then I need to figure out what I'm going to do with the rest of my life.

23

Chase

I'm GRINNING TO MYSELF, pacing and waiting for Bro when Parker flings my door open. It bounces off the wall and snaps off its hinges. "*You.*"

Mavis hustles after her. "She took down two security guards," she tells me, but unless I'm mistaken, there's more than a hint of pride in her voice. "Probably could've gotten four more."

"Damn right I could," Parker says.

I quit pacing and blink at both of them. My heart's suddenly in my throat. I should fire her, but she's Bro's best friend, and right now, I need to know this isn't about Bro. "Talk."

"The fucking *Bratwurst Wagon*? First you throw Vassar at her, and now the fucking Bratwurst Wagon."

My secretary looks like she wants a bowl of popcorn. I flick my wrist and give her the *get lost or get fired* glare.

Miraculously, it works.

She tries to shut the door, but it lists off its hinge and swings open again.

"What," I grit out, "are you talking about?"

"Oh, *please*. Who else is going to park the Bratwurst Wagon in front of our building?"

In three steps, I'm staring out the window at the street below.

Sure enough, there's the giant bratwurst on wheels, right across from the stretch Hummer I ordered. Bro told me yesterday after we got stuck in a weird position in the back of the Towncar that if she's going to blow me in a car, she's going to do it in a fucking stretch Hummer, so I got her a fucking stretch Hummer.

Swear to God, the mutant bratwurst wasn't parked there a minute ago.

"What the hell is that monstrosity doing on my street?" I growl.

"Exactly what you told it to do?" Parker suggests. "Torment Sia until she'd finally quit and leave you and your tar-ridden soul to run your little organic empire in peace?"

And there goes my heart, flopping and gasping about like a lake trout being eaten alive by mosquitoes. "Sit. Lose the attitude. And if someone doesn't fucking tell me what the hell *Vassar* means, I'm going to take away your beanbag chairs and replace them with vinyl bench seats made in China."

She gasps. "You wouldn't."

"Do you know what I am?" I say.

"A dick?" she guesses.

It's all I can do to not gouge out my own eyeballs. "A man. With good intentions but limited understanding of the female language. I also skipped mind-reading in college, so you're going to have to start speaking in words that make

141

sense, or I can't fucking fix this. Vassar. Now. What does it mean?"

She gapes at me. "You seriously don't know?"

I try to claw matching chunks out of my desk with my bare hands.

It doesn't work.

"Sia got kicked out of Vassar for the Bratwurst Wagon incident," she whispers. "She had to leave Minnesota and go live with some distant relative to go to community college in Pennsylvania after she did her nights in jail and community service hours."

I drop into my chair, an understanding of where I went wrong Friday night finally worming its way into my brain. Makes sense now why Google wasn't helpful.

She never made it there.

"How did you not know that?" she demands.

"I had a few other problems on my hands back then," I grit out. "Why's the Bratwurst Wagon parked out front?"

"I don't know. I thought you knew. You know there's a restraining order prohibiting Sia from getting within a hundred yards of it for the rest of her life, right?"

"That's not a thing."

"Yes, it is."

"A vehicle can't get a restraining order. *It's not human.*"

"You tell that to your backwoods Minnesota sheriff."

I shove to my feet again. "Where's Ambrosia?"

"If I knew that, do you think I'd be up here?"

My phone rings on my desk. Eight messages beep on my email. My cell sings some Aretha.

Mom's calling. Bro's gone. And I have to get rid of the Bratwurst Wagon.

"She told the whole department about what happened between you two," Parker says. She turns around. "And she didn't leave out *anything*. Serves you right. You never should've bought her store."

"I'm going to fix this," I tell her.

She shakes her head and frowns at me. "I don't think you can."

I want to argue, but I'm afraid she's right.

Where Bro's concerned, the only two things I'm good at are fucking her, and fucking her over.

Chase

I can't stop thinking about Bro. It's been a week, and she's gone. She hasn't been to work. She's not answering my calls or texts. IT tells me she's not reachable through internal messaging on her phone, which most likely means she's removed the app. Her formal resignation hasn't come in, but it's inevitable.

If Zeus and Ares know where she is, they either won't or can't tell me. There's no sign she's been back to her apartment, though the farm-animal-mating struggle on the floor above has been going on every single trip I've made to check.

Parker hasn't heard from her either. Nor have their other friends. Their band is in demand after the write-up on Page Six, but they can't book without Bro.

And I'm a fucking mess.

One minute I want to throttle her. The next I want to take her to bed and screw her brains out until neither of us can remember anything, from our history to our favorite insults to even our names.

My childhood was hell. My family was broke white trash, too rich for food stamps, too poor for anything but white bread and the canned baloney Mom brought home from work every week. My father had a problem. Several, actually. Any cash Mom didn't use or hide quickly enough was gambled away. Bro's family was my escape. I was still a nobody, but I was a nobody with somewhere to go.

To the rest of the world, now I'm somebody. I'll live in the white-collar world until the day I die. There's nothing my money can't buy, and no shortage to the people who want to know me.

But to Bro Berger, I'll always be that scrappy, angry twit who once tried to set her ponytails on fire. The guy who banged her inside a giant bratwurst. The jackass who cost her Vassar.

She doesn't trust me enough to believe I don't want to spend the rest of my life throwing it in her face.

And why would she?

"Honey, I don't understand your fascination with this woman," Mom is saying. I took two days off and flew halfway around the world to have lunch with her in Mykonos. Never doubt the power of maternal guilt. Or fresh baklava. "She tried to wreck your life."

I stare out over the sailboats dancing on the crystal waters of the Mediterranean, because despite being thirty years old and having enough money in the bank to buy this entire city, if not half the country, I can't quite look my mother in the eye. "Mom, she wasn't lying. I was there."

"I'm well aware, though we both wish I wasn't."

I give her a wry grin and go back to watching the sea. It's a little turbulent today.

Sort of like my life.

"Still," she says, "I know you didn't tell her to steal that thing."

I want to deny it, but I can't. I know Bro. I knew Bro then too.

There wasn't a single ounce of me surprised when she jumped into the driver seat and took off in that bratwurst. She has just as much of a twisted sense of adventures as her brothers. She's not as loud or obvious about it, but who is next to those two oafs?

I'd left the parking lot that night thinking that she was Bro Berger. Of course she'd talk her way out of any trouble she'd get into in the Bratwurst Wagon. She always had. Her parents would come to her rescue, she'd fake some tears for the police officers, and her little princess life would go on.

I'd gotten home to find my mother gray and unconscious on the floor, and I hadn't given Bro another thought for weeks. Mostly, anyway. After her brothers' ill-timed visit to defend her honor the next morning, followed by a visit with some questions from the cops, I'd decided she could rot in hell for all I cared. I hadn't known she'd basically been headed there.

I'd been in a hell of my own, watching my mother fight for her life.

"Chase Ryan Jett, tell me you didn't tell that girl to steal the Bratwurst Wagon."

"A wise woman once told me we can't change the past, we can only change the future."

She heaves a mother-sigh and sips at her coffee. "When did you get smart enough to throw my words back at me?"

"Smart enough to repeat 'em, not smart enough to know how to use them."

"You want her in your future."

"Doesn't matter. I'm not good for her."

Mom plunks her teacup down.

I hold up my hands before the lecture can start and tick my transgressions off on my fingers. "She got arrested at eighteen because of me. There was the elevator incident two weeks ago. The Kiss Cam. Don't ask about the Irish bar."

"The girl's troubled."

"She was never troubled, she was related to Zeus and Ares. She's been squeaky-clean the past ten years. Good student, then a dedicated employee. She went from small-town Minnesota girl to making New York City her oyster. Lots of friends. Then I show up, push a few buttons—" or she pushes a few buttons, like she did in the elevator "—and one or both of us loses our minds."

She sighs again. "I was like that with your father," she murmurs.

First, didn't need that visual, but I suppose I've given her a few she didn't care to have lately too. Second— "Exactly. The world's a better place if we're not together."

"You're not your father." She squeezes my hand. "Though she might be."

"Mom…"

"Those Berger boys have really surprised me." She's not subtle in changing the subject, which is fine with me. "They've found a productive way to channel all their energy. It's rather impressive."

"So I can go play with them after school?" I deadpan.

She laughs. "Don't let this give you any ideas, but I was glad you had them. Goodness knows what kind of criminal record you would've had if you'd run around with boys who weren't from such a good family. But your obsession with their sister… You've never been able to think straight when she's around."

She's not wrong.

"Oh, look, it's my friend, Iris." She leans up in her seat and waves. "Iris! Iris, come meet my son. He's the one I was telling you about."

She re-settles her floppy straw hat on her head as Iris turns to make her way toward us.

"Don't let the cane fool you," Mom says. "She's only fifty-eight, and she doesn't look a day over forty when she's up close and sitting down with her makeup on. Her husband left her a fortune, and even though she's through menopause, she's open to the idea of adopting. Which is good, because I want grandchildren."

I blink at the woman who gave birth to me. "You are *not* right."

"She won't break your heart. Or drive you to getting yourself arrested for indecent exposure on the Kiss Cam."

"Next time I book you a cruise, I'm buying out the rest of the boat and donating all the rooms to sorority girls on spring break."

"Oh, honey." She pats my cheek. "You'll have plenty of time for that after Iris is in a nursing home."

I open my mouth, but for once, my mother has left me speechless. She almost sounds serious.

Until she cackles with undisguised glee, that is. "My goodness, no wonder you were always pulling pranks. This is quite the power trip."

"Don't get used to it," I say. "Takes a lot to prank a prankster."

"Honey, I'm your mother. I know all your tricks and more." She ruins the straight face with another gleeful cackle.

I'm chuckling at the sheer joy in her laughter when my phone dings.

And nothing's funny anymore.

I know where Bro went.

And it's suddenly crystal clear just how much work I have to do if I want to win her back.

25

Ambrosia

I WILL NEVER, for as long as I live, understand why people think gossip happens in New York. You want gossip? Come to Wishberry Lake. These ladies could write columns that would put those Post columnists to shame.

And they have been.

All week.

Except the most exciting thing that usually happens in Wishberry Lake is someone catching The Appendicitis, or someone else running over a mailbox with their boat trailer, or yet another someone else subscribing to *Playboy*, which the entire town will know about in less time than it takes Tisha (who *used* to be in accounting but is now apparently in an unemployment line) to stretch her fingers over her keyboard.

And Tisha has some fast-stretching fingers.

The one thing Wishberry Lake does even better than the gossip?

Maternal guilt.

"All I'm saying, sweetheart, is that you stayed away for ten years. It's natural for people to be curious after such a long absence. Even if you weren't trying to do unspeakable things with the town billionaire on camera at Yankee Stadium."

I tie a blue gingham square around the lid of a mason jar engraved with *Ketchup is the Spice of Life* and briefly wonder if Hogzilla's mother ever gave her guilt trips for her life choices.

I miss my upstairs neighbor.

And not just because she'd be the only thing more interesting than me in Wishberry Lake's gossip train.

"Kristy Knutsy asked me if he used his billions for member enhancement. That's not curiosity. That's invasion of privacy."

"But not your privacy," she points out.

"I don't want people thinking about penises that I have or haven't touched, okay?" Yes, I know. I'm the girl who proposed sex rooms. But when I'm in Wishberry Lake, I get a touch of the prude.

No, I don't *touch the prude*. I get inflicted with the native prudishness. Jeez, people. Can't I make up a phrase without it getting as twisted as the Dick's dick?

I pinch my lips and suck in a big breath. Again.

My time in Wishberry Lake has pretty much consisted of sucking in big breaths, going out for fresh air and then retreating when one too many people give me the *She's been sleeping with Chase Jett again* looks, which are always accompanied by the swift belly glance of *I wonder if she's carrying the billionaire's baby*.

In case you're wondering, no one is blaming Chase for banging me. They might be questioning his judgment in sticking it in *me*—I'm a common criminal, don'tcha know, while he's the golden billionaire from Wishberry Falls, so who cares that he and those Berger boys who make millions playing hockey now once tried to use fishing line, hair spray, and a lighter to make a ring of fire around the lake and told people it was a ritualistic exorcism to rid me of PMS—but he's a man, and men think with their penises, honey.

If I thought it would do any good, I'd have Parker ship me a strap-on and I'd wear it around and tell people it's my new brain.

And as that thought strikes me, I pick up the next jar from Mom—this one engraved with *Lake Fed and Minnesota Bread*, and no, I don't know if she meant to spell it that way—and bang it against my forehead.

Which is the other thing I've been doing a lot this last week.

If I smack myself hard enough, I might give myself amnesia, and then I can pretend they're talking about some other Ambrosia when I go out in town. Being Drew Barrymore in *Fifty First Dates* doesn't seem like a bad fate today.

Mom sets aside her engraving tools. "Ambrosia, you know you were an accident."

"*MOM!*"

She shakes her head. "That came out wrong. We love you very much, sweetheart, and we're glad we have you. I just mean you weren't planned. By the time your brothers were six months old, we knew we had our hands full and that there was something not entirely normal about them. Frankly, your father and I were a bit concerned that our genes were incompatible, and we weren't sure we should risk unleashing more of our random genetic combinations on the human race. But you were sweet and perfect, and you slept through the night and never smeared poop on the walls or peed on the cat or shook your weewee at the mailman. You were so responsible, we didn't realize until too late that we might not have given you enough attention—god knows your brothers needed most of it—and that you might one day act out too."

I'm squeezing my eyes shut now, because I don't know if I want to hear more.

"And I fear we've screwed up again," she says. "If we'd pressed you harder to come home, this all would've blown over years ago. But we let you stay away. We let people think we were ashamed. We let this grow in everyone's imagination until it's bigger than it needed to be, and once again, you're paying for our mistakes."

I'm not sure if she just said I was paying for being an accident, or if she said they love me despite screwing me up, but I know I'm on emotional overload. I stand and hug her. "Love you, Mom." And then I take myself out the back door and start walking.

Eventually I end up on a quiet bench on the far side of the lake that our town is named after. There's nothing but farmland and giant mosquitoes behind me, the sparkling five-hundred-acre lake before me. There's also probably the mutant motorized tricycle-motorcycle thing Zeus and Chase tried to build when they were in high school buried in the muck down there under the water. Ares got mad when he was too big for it, so he flung it out into the middle of the lake.

That thing had to have weighed at least a hundred pounds, and Ares threw it like it was a little stone. I'd watched from the woods on the west side of the lake, awestruck by just how cool my brothers were.

Dad told me a bunch of tourists came and tried to scuba dive for it last summer after Zeus told the story during an interview, but all they found was a wheel and the remnants of a blow horn.

I surround myself with a fog of bug spray, tuck my knees up to my chin, duck my head, and close my eyes against the sun glittering off the lake and the slight chill blowing in.

I'm still awestruck by my brothers when I watch them on the ice. They might've traumatized me as a child, but they also made life fascinating. Especially when Chase was around.

He added a certain brand of finesse to their pranks and adventures. A dark, subtle undertone that said *Chase Jett was here, and you can suck his dick if you don't like it.*

I shiver. And not because my jacket is too light for the May wind, or because the non-organic bug spray is giving me seizures, or because my subconscious is trying to forever expel Chase's name from my pores.

I'm shivering because I don't want to forget.

I don't want to remember, but I don't want to forget.

Sometimes I wish I was Ares. I doubt he ever has conundrums. I know he can't spell it. Eats, Screws, and Leaves. That's Ares. With a little hockey and the occasional naptime thrown in.

Someone sits on the end of my bench, and all the little hairs on the back of my neck prickle to life.

There are three classes of people who would want to be publicly seen with me right now. There's my family, but they know when I want space. There are the gossips, but they do their best work without going straight to the source.

And then there are the guys who want to screw me.

I think that classification includes a list of exactly one person, and my hoo-ha gives a throb to demonstrate for me that his odorless pheromones are present.

Either that, or this is some freakish sexual bug spray.

I'm contemplating whether *sexual bug spray* should be a thing when he speaks. "My mom almost died of a massive heart attack the night of the Bratwurst Wagon."

A surprised gasp catches in my throat, but I don't look up.

Not yet.

"I was a big enough shithead that I probably would've denied everything that happened with you even I hadn't been sitting at her bedside in the hospital while she was recovering from an emergency quadruple bypass, but that's why I didn't know what happened with Vassar. And I'm sorry. For whatever that's worth."

He apologized, my hopeless vagina squeals. *Let's hump him.*

She's on probation, so I ignore her.

But I tilt my head toward Chase. Just a little. Barely enough to make out his chiseled profile. His hands hanging between his knees, shoulders hunched forward, a touch of glitter still sparkling on his cheek, eyes on the lake.

We all went skating on the lake once. Chase stole my favorite doll and taunted me with her all afternoon, skating just fast enough—backwards, the bastard—to keep her out of my reach.

I'd been too young to sneak over to his house and set fire to his underwear in retaliation, but I'd had a pretty intricate plan built up when my brothers did something else to distract me.

I'm almost smiling.

My childhood was freaking *fun*.

"Insurance didn't come close to covering all the bills," Chase continues. "Doctors told her to quit eating canned baloney, and that she'd need at least six months off work because she shouldn't stand in the factory for eight to ten hours a day right after heart surgery. Disability barely covered the bills. I went head-down looking for a way to take care of her. Being a shithead and playing video games were all I had, so that's where I went."

Now my heart's getting into it. *He was twenty, Bro. Twenty years old and responsible for his mom's hospital bills. He wasn't there for you because he was doing something more noble.*

"Yeah, well, prison sucked too," I say.

He ducks his head, but I see him sucking in a smile. "Couldn't have been too bad. That prison tattoo on your ass is almost spelled right."

There's no prison tattoo and he knows it. I give him a halfhearted backhand to the biceps, at which point my limbs jump on team Chase too. *God, he's hot. Can we touch him some more?*

"I didn't order the Bratwurst Wagon last week." He's staring me straight in the eye now, power and truth radiating from his focused gaze. "I wouldn't do that to you. Even if I hated you like I hate canned baloney, I wouldn't do that to you."

I believe him.

And not just because everything from my vagina to my fingers to my heart wants me to, or because I've realized I might've made a few enemies at work who could've Googled me just as easily as my friends had, once they knew what to look for.

"Do you hate me like you hate canned baloney?" I whisper.

I think I've always known Chase Jett was a beautiful specimen of a man, and I've always taken a perverse pleasure in denying it. But watching him battle a smile at my expense is melting me, and not just in places that I want him to touch me with his mouth and his penis.

"No, Bro, I don't hate you like I hate canned baloney."

"Canned tuna?"

"Or canned tuna."

"Canned mushrooms?"

He sucks in a thoughtful breath and peers out over the lake. "That might be getting closer. Canned mushrooms are an abomination. I might hate you like I hate canned mushrooms."

He loves canned mushrooms. The disgusting fucker used to sit at my parents' kitchen table and inhale them like Ares eats saltwater taffy. And then he'd drink the juice straight out of the can.

"Yeah, well, I hate you like I hate boy bands," I grumble as I rock my hips sideways and angle closer to him.

He drapes an arm over the back of the bench. His fingers brush my neck, and a delicious shiver races down my spine. "I hate you like I hate skiing in the Alps."

I haven't fully explored his thighs yet. I give the closest one a firm squeeze. My center ignites like a blowtorch. "I hate you like I hate pineapple tater tot casserole."

He arches a brow at me. "Usually I get turned on when you say disgusting things to me."

"You have the taste of a hunchbacked mountain troll and your hand is so limp you can't even jack yourself off." I slap a hand over my mouth, because I'm in Wishberry Lake and Wishberry Lake Bro is hornified that I'd say such a thing out loud.

But Chase tips his head back and laughs deep and long, and I realize his laugh isn't the only thing going long. Nor is it the only thing I want going deep.

"We're really fucked up," I whisper.

He cradles my head into the crook of his neck. "I hate you like I hate pussy," he murmurs.

My pussy roars to life and demands a ride on the pony, but public fornication hasn't ever actually done anything good for me.

So I'm not sure why I'm leaping to straddle him, grabbing his cheeks in my palms while I center myself over that thick, hard, crooked, delicious rocket in his pants. "I hate you like I hate breathing," I say. "And I hate myself for that." I rock against him. The bench wobbles. "And for this too." I rock once more, and suddenly I'm flying forward, Chase backwards, as the whole bench flips.

We land with a thud. My legs are trapped under the wood, and I mean the wood of the bench, and "*Ow!*"

"Fuck!" Chase hisses. He twists, but every time he moves, my legs get crushed a little more. "Shit."

Unfortunately, every time he twists, he's also rubbing his bulge against my hoo-ha. "You need to stop," I gasp. "You need to stop *right now*."

His eyes meet mine, and understanding dawns. A slow smile spreads over his perfect, bitable lips. "Ambrosia May Berger, are you turned on?" he murmurs.

"I'm fucking stuck under this bench," I whisper.

He slips a finger into my pants, and I go cross-eyed. "We're in public. *Again*."

"I hate you like I hate doing you in public."

"I hate you like I hate orgasms."

He finds that perfect spot inside my panties, and thinking is suddenly overrated.

And that's exactly how my mother finds us ten seconds later.

26

Chase

OTHER THAN NEVER BEING ABLE TO look Dr. Berger in the eye again, today's going pretty well. Bro's talking to me. Her legs aren't broken. Neither is my back. And we're heading in to talk to the police chief.

"For the record, I am two seconds from texting Eloise and asking her to spread a picture of your diseased dick all over the internet," she hisses as I drag her along.

"You don't have any pictures of my dick," I murmur.

"Doesn't matter. Everyone knows I'm in your pants. Plausibility is all I need to ruin your sex life forever."

"My sex life is with you. I don't care what you tell the world about my penis."

She's getting the eyeball of disbelief from her mother, the chief, and the chief's secretary. "Ambrosia, we *do not* talk about men's penises," her mother hisses.

"First of all, he's talking about his penis too. And second

of all, you wouldn't blink if he talked about my vagina," she hisses back.

All this hissing is getting annoying.

"I could talk about her vagina if you'd like," I offer.

The chief clears his throat and gives me the *don't be a sexual predator* look.

I remember this guy. Met him a time or two the last twenty years, mostly in my teenage years, usually accompanied by the Berger twins. He's a thinner and grayer on top now, thicker around the middle, and more bow-legged in his gait. When he gestures us into his office, Bro's trembling.

I squeeze her hand.

"Mr. Jett," the chief says, "what can we do for you today?"

"*Mr. Jett,*" Bro mutters.

"You can call me dickhead," I tell the chief. "All my best friends do."

Bro snorts. She's shaking still, but I suspect it's turning into a good shake.

"My grandchildren are going to be brainless delinquents," Dr. Berger sighs.

"Zeus might come through for you, ma'am," I offer.

Bro snort-cackles, and I turn to the chief. "I'm here to turn myself in," I announce.

Bro chokes on her snort-cackle. The chief gives me a bored *quit wasting my time* look. "For what?"

"Defacing and attempted robbery of an official visiting vehicle of Baloney Fest ten years ago."

Bro sinks into a chair. She's blinking almost as fast as her chest is rising and falling.

I hope my bank account can write me a check out of this, because I have plans for that woman. Tonight. Tomorrow. Every hour for the next month, year, decade.

The chief looks between me and Bro. "The statute of

limitations has run out on any crimes that may have occurred ten years ago."

I hold out my wrists. "I insist you arrest me. Now."

"Mr. Jett—"

"Dickhead," I correct. "I terrorized this town for almost twenty years, and I left it after doing heinously unspeakable things to an honored vehicular guest. We don't need to stand on formality simply because I made a few bucks."

He rubs his forehead. "Son, I can't arrest you."

"There are very few people in this town who would've claimed me as a son before I was a billionaire."

Bro grabs my wrist and tugs my hand down. "Chase. Stop. This isn't necessary."

I fucking love it when she says my name. "Either you arrest me, or you clear Ambrosia's record," I say.

No one's laughing now, and Dr. Berger has joined Bro, squishing into the same chair with her daughter like her sons used to squeeze into a single bus seat.

The chief glances between me and Bro. "It's an honorable thing you're doing, son, but the law's the law."

I hunch over the chief's desk, resting on my knuckles. "The law fucked up, and one person took the fall for two people's crimes. You're going to tell me the quickest way to solve this, or I'll be calling a press conference to discuss *every* case this office has mishandled in the last twenty years."

Two-thirds of those cases involve officers letting me and the Berger boys off with warnings for shit we should've been jailed for. They put me in front of a camera, I'm spilling it all. And if you think the Twin Tanks won't be tripping over themselves to make up even more shit than we actually did, you don't know them very well.

Judging by the way the chief is turning green at the gills but purple everywhere else, he knows it too. "Let me make a few phone calls," he grits out.

Bro gasps. She slugs me in the back, which I interpret to mean *thank you, you ugly, rich bastard*.

Inspiration strikes. "While you're doing that, is your holding cell empty?"

"Joe Gus Johnson's back there. Caught him terrorizing a hog last night."

"Why is it always the hogs?" Bro mutters.

"I'm sorry," Dr. Berger interrupts, "but did you just say he was fornicating with a pig?"

"Don't say sorry," Bro hisses at her.

"That's the charge, ma'am."

"A man was caught with his peepee in a pig, and *my daughter* is the one they're gossiping over?" She leaps to her feet, bends over the desk, and grabs the chief by the earlobe. *"Why is no one talking about this man corrupting a sheep?"*

"Hog," I correct.

Bro snuffle-snorts like her upstairs neighbors back in the city, and I almost lose my shit.

"Ma'am, I don't control the gossip," the chief says. "Please unhand me before I *do* have to arrest someone in this room. Namely, you."

"Give it a good tweak first, Mom," Bro says.

She drops the chief and shoves herself to the door. "Excuse me. I have gossip to spread. And a subpoena to file for any pictures you might have."

"I'm going to need you to release Joe Gus on bail," I tell the chief. "And I need to use the holding pen. With the cameras turned off. And the doors locked."

"Chase," Bro whispers. "You are *not* putting yourself in jail."

"Nope. I'm putting *us* in jail."

27

Ambrosia

CHASE JETT IS CERTIFIABLY insane and I'm going to kick his ass and gouge his eyeballs out and claw at that dimple in his chin until it's the only thing left of his chin, because *the fucker just got me thrown back in jail.*

The door clinks shut, trapping us behind unbreakable steel bars. I'm doing my best not to hyperventilate, because I can't destroy him if I can't breathe, when he starts unbuttoning his shirt.

It's a soft blue, and it makes his eyes extra bright. It also feels like a velvet silk, and concentrating on his long, capable fingers on the small buttons is the only thing keeping me from hitting the cold, hard concrete floor.

"*What the ever-loving unholy* fuck *are you doing?*" I shriek.

He wiggles his eyebrows. "Getting ready for my strip search."

"This is *so* not funny," I hiss, but not all of me is in complete agreement with my mouth's assessment.

Parts of me are waking up and showing completely inappropriate interest.

His shirt flutters to the ground, leaving him in a sleeveless white undershirt tucked into his black jeans. His arms are sculpted beauty, his shoulders broad and bitable, his hips tight, his zipper bulging.

He makes quick work of pulling off the undershirt, and my mouth goes dry.

I've lost track of the number of orgasms this man has given me, but aside from that afternoon in my shower, I've never had a chance to fully appreciate his entire body in fully fluorescent lighting.

He kicks off his shoes, then shucks himself out of his pants and briefs in one swift motion. My legs suddenly can't support me. I sink to the metal cot behind me and drink him in.

Shoulders of a god. Copper nipples nestled in a wavy matte of dark hair. His biceps need their own zip code, and his forearms are corded steel.

I want to lick his six-pack and sink my fingers into that beautiful man-vee perfectly showcasing his strong, curved shaft as it strains toward me. *Hello, beautiful, I've missed you.*

His thighs are powerful, and when I crook a finger at him, he bends and captures my mouth with his.

This kiss is everything. Licking, suckling, nipping, teasing, but not battling. His hands slide over my body, soothing and arousing at the same time. I stroke his bare shoulders, flick my fingers at his nipples, trace his abs, and finally rake my fingers down his cock.

He groans in my mouth, and suddenly he's lifting me off the cot and carrying me to the back of the cell.

I cling to his shoulders. "What are you doing?"

"Swear to god, baby, I'm thinking beautiful, filthy things right now, but I don't want to know where that thing's been."

I start laughing, but then my back hits cold cinderblocks. He shifts me so my legs are wrapped around his hips, his rod rubbing my clit, and rational thought evaporates.

"I don't hate fucking you," I pant.

"I fucking love fucking you," he rasps.

"Did they turn the cameras off?"

"If they didn't, I'll kill 'em."

We're locked in a jail cell, Chase is naked as a jaybird, threatening law enforcement officers, and I'm so turned on that I'm one big pulsing ball of lust.

"Too many clothes," I say. "Off. Now."

He helps me rip off my shirt while I rub my pussy all over his dick. Breaking contact with him physically hurts, but he holds my gaze the whole time we're yanking my pants off, and I know he's going to make it better.

He's going to fill me and stretch me and hit all those good places to make me fall apart, and then he's going to kiss me silly and do it all over again. All night long. With his mouth. With his hands. With his amazing supercock.

My leg comes free from my pants, and I practically climb him to get back to where I want to be. Where I *need* to be.

I don't give him a chance to touch me, to get me off with his fingers or his tongue. I don't want foreplay. I want *him*. I *need* him. I need him inside me, one with me, filling me and joining me and completing me.

"Bro," he gasps as I slide down his length, and *oh my god* I love the way he says my name. That he has his own nickname for me. That he's *mine*.

I don't care if we're a little fucked up. I don't care if I've hated him most of my life. I don't care if I lose my job or if I never go back to New York.

I just care that I'm his and he's mine.

My legs tighten around him as he pumps into me. He's huge, long and thick, and I can feel every heavy, solid inch of him on every thrust, and it's driving me mad. I feel thick too. I'm heavy inside, building, coiling, desperate. With every drive, he hits that magic spot deep inside me where I ache the most, driving me higher, faster, faster and higher and deeper and spiraling out of control.

I'm panting his name, biting his ear, squeezing his nipples, his solid ass, and I'm about to come, *so* close, almost there, holy *Christ* he's so fucking big and perfect and twisted just right to—*ooooh*, yes yes *yes YES*.

I fall over the edge, all semblance of smooth moves gone as I jerk and writhe and squeeze, wave after wave of pleasure exploding from my core against his thick cock. I grab his face and tug his mouth to mine, licking and sucking on his tongue while he groans and pulses inside me, driving into me while we crash over the waves together until my body has no more to give.

My legs are jelly, and the frantic kisses have slowed to long, slow, languid licks. Our bodies are both slicked with sweat, and I've completely forgotten that we're in a jail cell.

Until now.

I tense, and Chase wraps his arms around me. "You're fucking beautiful," he says against my cheek, his lips tickling and teasing my skin.

I squeeze his hips with my legs, or try anyway—jelly doesn't squeeze well.

Still, his cock pulses deep inside me. It's like his penis is a sex triathlete, though the only events it better be competing in are my mouth and my vagina. So…a sex biathlete?

No, wait. He can come in my hand too.

If he has to.

"Naughty minx," he murmurs.

"You have no idea," I reply.

"Bro?" he says.

"Mm?"

"Congratulations. We just made prison our bitch."

He gives me the most adorable grin I've ever seen. My body is sated, my freak-out button has been completely deactivated, and this handsome, evil, brilliant, twisted man with his dick still twitching in my hoo-ha is smiling at me.

I tip my head back and laugh, because what else is a jailbird to do after she's made prison her bitch?

Ambrosia

SIX YEARS AGO, I arrived in New York with a criminal record, a bachelor's degree from a second-rate college, and a chance from a small, local, organic grocery chain.

Today, I land back in my city with my record erased, a promise that I'll be given a fair chance at promotion in the same grocery store, and a billionaire boyfriend whom I gave my virginity to on the floor of the Bratwurst Wagon one memorable night shortly after I graduated high school.

Oh, and I've officially joined the mile high club.

Twice.

My brothers are overjoyed. Not about the mile high club —there are some things they don't need to know—but that Chase is back in their lives. My parents were bought with new golf clubs (Dad) and a shiny new website with full tech support and direct sales options (Mom). My all-girl boy band cover band bandmates are saving their judgment until we see if we can get through an entire two weeks without getting arrested for public indecency.

As my hoo-ha says, there are worse things to get arrested for than good orgasms.

We swing by my apartment to grab my goldfish and aloe plant—okay, yes, and to have a quickie—and don't even make it in the door before the dust starts flaking down from the ceiling.

Squeaky-squeaky-squeaky-squeeeeeeeeak...

Chase and I look at each other, and we both crack up. Joe Gus Johnson is currently in hiding back in Wishberry Lake, riding high on the notoriety that kept me away for ten years, thanks to my mother's righteous indignation fueling her dip into the gossip waters.

Also helping redirect the gossip? Chase announced that he was buying the baloney factory and converting it to Crunchy's Midwestern regional headquarters, with on-the-job cross-training opportunities for employees who wanted to stay through the transition. No lay-offs, full paychecks without pause. Pending my criminal record being obliterated by local law enforcement, of course.

I think I might seriously feel something way stronger than not-hate for this man.

Have no fear—the Baloney Festival will still go on, though he's threatening to set up a tofaloney booth. Either way, the Bratwurst Wagon has been permanently disinvited.

Hogzilla's battle cry echoes through the ceiling of my apartment, accompanied by a wolf howl.

Chase peers curiously at the ceiling. "I honestly want to know what's actually going on up there."

"I don't usually hate your sick sense of adventure," I tell him.

"You were much more complimentary about my sense of

adventure two hours ago when we were in the air," he says with a smirk.

I don't hate that smirk either. And I kind of love that there's *still* a fleck of glitter next to his lip.

"Oh, please," I say with a smile I couldn't suppress even if I wanted to. "I was trying not to yawn the whole time. You know what altitude does to your wrinkled pickle."

He catches me around the waist and hefts me over his shoulder. "I'll show you a *wrinkled pickle*, woman." He lugs me around the screen to my bed and stops short. "You have got to be fucking kidding me."

I suddenly know what he's seeing, and I feel my face go bright red. "I don't hate when you fuck me on my couch," I stutter.

"Oh, no," he says. "If you're still using a boy band blanket, I'm going to fuck you on your boy band blanket."

Yes, yes, my bed is a shrine to the boy band Bro Code. I know I should quit them—they broke up like a decade ago—but of all the boy bands of my youth, they were the hottest. "It's a *comforter*, not a blanket. And it's my inspiration for my budding musical career."

He tosses me onto the boy band and quickly covers my body with his, his fingers finding my nipples. "I don't hate your boy band cover band," he says while he takes aim at my neck with his teeth.

I grip his hair, spread my legs, and tilt my head to give him better access. "I don't hate your huge, swollen, wrinkled pickle."

He thrusts said pickle at me through our clothes, and I attack him like a rabid bunny in need of a good fuck. Clothes go flying, his hands are all over my skin, his mouth headed to the promised land. "You make me crazy, Bro," he tells my pussy.

He licks me with one long, languid stroke, and I buck my hips up into his mouth. "We're fucking insane," I gasp.

Except I know we're not. Turns out, when we're not fighting or fucking, we have a lot in common. We both want to make the world a better place through food. We both love music. And we both love doing filthy things to each other that would make even my brothers blush.

Wait. That's still the fucking.

But it's *so* good.

His magic fingers slide into me while his tongue flicks my clit, and just like that, I'm clenching and spasming and doing my own mating call. This man just *knows* me.

He kisses his way back up my body, teasing me with his thick, delicious cock. He's holding me captive with his eyes, determined and dark and intense, and my heart squeezes.

This man has all of me.

"I don't hate the way I love you," he whispers.

I roll us so I'm on top, sliding down his length, taking all of him into me as deep as he'll go. I stroke the stubble on his cheeks, play my fingers down his neck and across his collar-bone. "I don't hate the way I love you either."

"Show me," he says.

And I do.

For the rest of my life, I do.

EPILOGUE

Bro (But only to her lover—everyone else calls her Sia. Or Ambrosia if they're family.)

THERE ARE three things I love: these organic chocolate chip cookies the lady in the snack bar got me addicted to, a good prank, and Chase Jett.

But mostly I love Chase Jett.

Shocking, right? And he didn't even pay me to say that. Not that I'd take his filthy money. I know where it's been. I'd tell you all about it, but there are *some* things a girl likes to keep between her and her lover.

Tonight, he's hanging by the wall in the basement of a library not far from the office, bopping his head along to the music while the girls and I rock out at a retirement party. I'm ignoring his *speed it up so we can sneak into the stacks upstairs* bedroom eyes, and only partly because I'm a musical professional.

Mostly, though, because I love the way he growls and

attacks me—in the good way, of course—when I've made him wait.

I wink at him and turn my attention back to our audience. These ladies know how to let their hair down and party. So does their surprise guest, who just happens to be this stripper Parker's been obsessed with since we took her to Studmuffins for her birthday.

His mother's the retiree of honor. And it's obvious where he got his moves. Weird that a stripper has a librarian for a mother, but hey, my mother's a university professor and she got my brothers. Who am I to judge?

We're almost done with our last set, and as we go into "I Do (Cherish You)" by 98 Degrees, Chase shoots me one of his *You're going to owe me* looks. But I know he doesn't actually mind dancing with Judy's mother, especially since her walker leaves plenty of room between them for the holy ghost.

He's actually quite charming with people when he's not trying to put worms in their peanut butter sandwiches.

Who knew?

We finish up the song to a round of applause, Willow thanks everyone for being such a great audience and wishes Judy a wonderful retirement, and I make quick work of packing up my keyboard.

"Seriously, Sia?" Parker says. She's still sporting a blush that hasn't gone away since the stripper entered the building, but that doesn't stop her from telegraphing that she knows *exactly* what's on my mind. "In a *library*?"

"Speed it up, Bro." Chase steps up behind me and settles his hand on my lower back, and I get tingles all over my skin and a surge of primal lust settles hard and heavy in my core. "I want to check out the comic books before we go."

"If you ruin Tarzan…" Parker says.

"Go on, you two." Willow shoos us. "Be quick and don't get caught."

"Willow!" Parker hisses.

"What? They're gonna do it anyway, might as well get it over with before anyone else catches on."

I don't hear Parker's counter-argument, because Chase is tugging me to the stairwell. "Your band doesn't suck," he tells me.

I swat him on the ass. "Watching you watch us doesn't suck either."

He grins back at me and bypasses the first floor. Then the second. And the third. We finally emerge on the roof of the library, where there's a small table set with champagne and chocolate covered strawberries, the soft sounds of OneRepublic blending in with the summer city night, and fairy lights strung around the half-wall.

It's beautiful and romantic and my heart is utterly melting.

"Who are you, and what have you done with my boyfriend?" I ask Chase as I wrap my arms around his neck.

"What? This? It's for my other girlfriend."

I laugh as I pepper his jaw with kisses. "Is she hotter than me?"

"Way hotter." His hands are trailing up my back under my shirt. They stop mid-way, and I know he's suddenly realized I'm not wearing a bra.

"Does she sing better?" I ask.

"Yes. And no man has ever had to break her piano to save anyone's ears."

I'm laughing again, but his hands slide around my front to cradle my breasts, and my breath catches.

"I love touching you." He grazes my earlobe with his teeth, pokes me in the belly with his rock-hard cock, and once again, this man has turned me into a giant mass of raging pheromones and lust. "And seeing you smile. And watching you play. And making you come."

And now I'm all warm and glowy in my heart, which makes being turned on even hotter. "I love loving you," I whisper.

He captures my mouth with his while I make quick work of undoing his button. He takes me hot and hard and fast against a brick wall on the roof, touching me in all my favorite places while I scrape my nails over all *his* favorite places, his mouth on mine, his tongue feasting on mine, his solid cock sliding in and out of my pussy, filling me and teasing me and completing me, until I shatter into a million happy stars and take him over the edge with me.

His fingers twirl in my hair as we both catch our breath. "I love you, Ambrosia May Berger," he tells my shoulder.

I stroke the back of his neck and pull him closer.

We might not have a normal love story, but it's ours.

Because Chase Jett—this man who comes to hear my band play, who dances with little old ladies, and who makes love to me on impromptu rooftop dates—is worth every challenge we've been through.

And I wouldn't change any of it for the world.

ABOUT THE AUTHOR

Pippa Grant is a stay-at-home mom and housewife who loves to escape into sexy, funny stories way more than she likes perpetually cleaning toothpaste out of sinks and off toilet handles. When she's not reading, writing, sleeping, or trying to prepare her adorable demon spawn to be productive members of society, she's fantasizing about chocolate chip cookies.

Find Pippa at...

www.pippagrant.com
pippa@pippagrant.com

COPYRIGHT

Made in United States
Orlando, FL
15 March 2024

44810575R00114